Searching

New Beginnings Book 3

ROBIN MERRILL

New Creation Publishing
Madison, Maine

SEARCHING. Copyright © 2021 by Robin Merrill. All rights reserved. No part of this book may be used or reproduced in any manner whatsoever without written permission except in the case of brief quotations embodied in critical articles and reviews.

Scripture quotations taken from Darby Translation.

This novel is a work of fiction. Names, characters, businesses, organizations, places, events, and incidents are either the products of the author's imagination or used in a fictitious manner. Any resemblance to actual persons, living or dead, or actual events is purely coincidental.

And these were more noble than those in Thessalonica, receiving the word with all readiness of mind, daily searching the scriptures if these things were so.
—Acts 17:11

Chapter 1
Levi

"Why are we stopping here?" Something in Levi's stomach churned.

In the front seats of the banged-up Chevy Cruze, Kendall and Shane exchanged a look that intensified Levi's foreboding. "We told you," Kendall said. "It's a surprise."

Levi looked out his window. "Yeah, but there's nothing here."

"Exactly." Kendall laughed as if he'd said something funny and swung his door open. It clunked against a boulder, but Kendall didn't care. He had no emotional attachment to his car. Or to anything else.

Annoyed, Levi also got out of the car and went to stand beside Kendall. They were in a sort of clearing. Levi thought it was probably an old logging landing. His eyes scanned the bushes and landed on a sun-faded plastic gas can. Yep, probably a landing.

Beyond this landing was nothing but forest. If loggers had cut it, they had only cut some of the trees.

Shane joined them. "There's nothing here because this is only a shortcut."

Searching

Great. A shortcut to a mystery location. This just kept getting better.

Shane slung his tattered backpack over his shoulder, and bottles clinked together.

"I thought we were coming out here to get high?"

Shane laughed. "We are. Nobody said I couldn't drink too."

Levi didn't like drunk Shane. High Shane was hilarious, but drunk Shane did stupid stuff. Stuff that could easily get them a ride in an ambulance. Or the backseat of a police car. Probably Shane would luck out and get the ambulance ride, leaving Levi with the cop car. "All right. Show me what you're gonna show me." He wanted to get high and then get on with his evening. He liked his friends, but he preferred to spend his Friday evenings with girls.

"Patience!" Kendall started walking.

The sun dipped behind the trees, and the shadows turned into real darkness. They were halfway across the landing when Levi rolled his ankle. "Ah," he cried and then wished he hadn't made a noise. Kendall and Shane weren't the most sympathetic and were more likely to poke fun than to have compassion. He couldn't see where he was walking. He needed light. He reached for his phone in his back pocket—but it wasn't there. He swore and stopped walking. He turned back toward the road. The car looked really far away.

"What?" Kendall sounded impatient.

"I forgot my phone."

"Come on." They kept walking. "You won't need it."

Levi hesitated.

"What, were you planning on taking some haunted house selfies?" Shane let out a peal of laughter. He was his own biggest fan.

"Haunted house? What haunted house?"

"It's not haunted," Kendall said, his tone implying that Shane was an immature fool for saying such a thing. "But it *is* creepy. Super creepy."

"And that makes you want to go get high there?" Levi's bad feeling wasn't going away.

"Absolutely. It's a trip. I've done it before. Trust me."

Levi did trust his friends. That was the problem. So he followed them toward the woods, further from the road, and deeper into the darkness.

They entered the trees, and then Levi couldn't see anything. The woods were thick with night sounds. Levi wasn't much of an outdoorsman and wasn't comfortable with his current circumstances. How had he been so stupid to leave his phone in the car? He couldn't even remember taking it out of his pocket. It must have fallen out.

"Almost there," Kendall said, and minutes after that, they spilled out onto what looked like a very old road.

Levi looked both ways. This road was too narrow to be a road. "Is this someone's driveway?"

"Used to be," Kendall said.

"Then why didn't we just drive up it?" A reasonable question, he thought.

"Because then someone might see our car," Kendall said as if Levi were several steps beyond stupid.

They followed the driveway up a small slope. The night was still loud, but Levi felt better now that his immediate surroundings had opened up a bit. He still had no idea where he was, but there wasn't much chance of getting lost. They were on a peninsula, so if he walked in a straight line, he would eventually hit either ocean or Bucksport.

"There it is." Kendall sounded reverent.

Levi looked up. The outline of an old house stood ahead of them. It *did* look a little haunted, though it wasn't like one of the haunted mansions in the horror movies where cute cheerleaders ran from room to room trying to escape ax-wielding ghosts. This was more like a haunted shack. And he didn't want to go anywhere near it. In fact, something inside him was screaming at him not to go any closer. "Come on, man." He stopped walking. "This is stupid." He no longer cared that much about getting high. And his ankle hurt.

"Fine." Kendall didn't even slow down. "Stay down here. But we're not afraid, so we're going to keep going. We'll be back eventually."

Levi didn't know what to do. He didn't want to go near that house. He didn't want to stay alone in the wilderness either. And they were only minutes away from full dark.

He started walking again.

The house got a little bigger when they drew near but only a little. Graffiti spattered the front wall. Kendall stepped onto the small porch, and it creaked under his weight. He shined his phone flashlight on the front door, which had an upside down star painted on the front of it. The red paint was faded, so it must have happened a while ago. Levi tried to find comfort in this. Some kid had painted the symbol on the door as a joke and then gone on to become a lawyer or doctor or something. That's all this was: kids messing around. Nothing more sinister than that.

Chapter 2
Levi

The abandoned house smelled like mold and urine. The back of Levi's hand went to his mouth. He was glad it was dark so that his friends wouldn't see this and call him a wuss.

"Shine your light over here," Shane said.

Levi dropped his hand.

Kendall pointed his phone at Shane's backpack, which he'd set on the floor. Shane unzipped the bag and pulled out a camping lantern.

When he lit it, the soft light felt brilliant compared to the darkness they'd been in. It brought Levi significant comfort. This will all be over soon, he told himself.

"Good idea." Kendall turned off his flashlight app. "Want to save my battery in case we can't find our way back to the car." He laughed as if this were hysterical.

Levi didn't find it the least bit funny. He surveyed his surroundings. They were in what had probably once been a kitchen. The inner walls were also covered in graffiti, most of it red and black. Previous partiers hadn't been big on color variety. Part of the ceiling had fallen in, and chunks of insulation lay on the floor. Based on the smell, Levi wondered if cats had lived there at some point. Or maybe they still did. This thought made him miss his cat, miss his trailer. He complained about that trailer often, was even embarrassed by it, but it was home. Maybe he should've stayed there tonight. Tucked in safe, warm, and bored. His mom would've been thrilled. He looked at Shane and was relieved to see that he didn't appear to be having much fun either.

"Come on." Kendall stomped through the room as if he'd been there a million times. With what friends, Levi had no idea. Kendall didn't have many.

Shane followed Kendall, and gingerly, Levi followed Shane.

The next room contained a few couches that, while old and filthy, didn't look as far gone as the rest of the house. Without reservation, Kendall plopped down on one of them. Shane soon followed. Levi didn't want to sit. He didn't want to catch something. And the air felt damp. He wasn't confident the couches were even dry.

"Hand me the plate," Kendall ordered.

Shane put his backpack on the floor, unzipped it again, and pulled out a plate and a straw.

Kendall pulled a plastic baggie out of his pocket. It was full of light brown powder. Levi didn't know what it was, but he didn't think it was good. He stepped closer for a better look. "Why'd you already crush up the pills?"

"I didn't. This isn't Percocet." He sprinkled a line out onto the tray and then used his ATM card to straighten it out.

"What is it?"

"It's dirt." Kendall finally looked up at Levi. "I told you we were going to have a good time."

Heroin? Levi was stunned. He was not about to do heroin. That stuff got you hooked after one try, and he didn't want to get hooked on heroin. Nor did he want to pass out in this creepy house.

Kendall picked up a straw and snorted the line. Then he let out a long breath and closed his eyes.

Levi's mouth watered. He wanted to feel some of what Kendall was feeling.

Shane greedily snatched the tray and baggie out of Kendall's lap. Smiling, Kendall didn't object. Shane did the same thing Kendall had done, though he seemed less comfortable with the process. Had Shane ever done heroin? Where had Kendall even gotten heroin? This was Carver Harbor, for crying out loud.

Searching

Shane snorted the line, dropped the straw, and stared straight ahead.

It seemed they had forgotten about Levi entirely.

This might be a good thing, Levi thought.

He sat on the other couch and then reached out and stealthily dragged Shane's backpack across the floor. The floor had been so wet for so long that it was almost slimy, and the pack slid more easily than Levi had thought it would. He rooted around in it until he found a bowl and some weed. Then he grew impatient when he couldn't find a lighter. He didn't want to ask them, though, because that would call attention to how he wasn't doing the dirt.

Finally, he found the lighter, and he packed the bowl. Then he flicked a flame into being and took a huge hit. He held it in his lungs for as long as he could, which was a fairly long time thanks to all his practice, and then exhaled. Then he looked around the room. The wallpaper was peeling and in some sections had been ripped entirely off. Some of it lay in chunks on the floor. There were actual holes in the wall, and Levi couldn't imagine why someone had wanted to put them there. He looked down at the bowl. He knew it would be more fun to take his time with it, but he wanted to catch up to his friends, so he took another hit.

It hit him, and his mouth spread into a lazy grin. There. That was more like it.

He took another hit and waited to feel it.

And boy, did he.

Maybe too much. His mind started darting to bad places. As he tried to calm his thoughts, his eyes landed on the holes in the walls. Maybe those hadn't been put there by someone on the outside. Maybe something *inside* the walls had broken out. Wait. That was insane. He shook his head as if trying to physically shake such thoughts out of his skull. He didn't need to be thinking crazy things like that. Why *was* he thinking crazy things like that? Was it something about this house? Or had there been something else in that weed? He looked into the bowl, but of course, the resin didn't tell him much. He pictured black creatures crawling out of the walls. This pot had been laced with something, he knew it. He looked at Shane. "Hey, what's in the weed?"

Kendall laughed. "What?" He opened his eyes. "Why you stealing Shane's weed?"

Shane gave no indication that he had heard them.

Kendall elbowed him in the ribs. "Hey, wake up, buddy. You got anything extra in that weed?"

Shane shook his head without opening his eyes. "I'm not sleeping, man. Obviously."

It wasn't obvious. Shane was drooling. The lantern cast an eerie light on Shane's face, making him look grotesque. Suddenly, Levi *knew* that Shane knew about the things in the wall. Levi stood up. "I'm outta here, man."

"What?" Kendall's head tipped forward. "Why, what'sa matta?" he mumbled.

Levi started toward the kitchen. He heard rustling behind him. Someone was following him. He picked up speed, and his right big toe caught on something hard. He staggered forward, slamming his left foot into the floor as he tried not to fall. There was a loud crack, and before Levi could wonder what that noise meant, it was replaced by a squishy popping sound that reminded him of someone walking through deep mud.

And then the floor gave way.

He was falling. His feet went first, but then his foot caught on something. At first he thought this was a good thing, but as the rest of him pitched downward, an unbelievable pain tore through his ankle and up his leg, and he knew nothing was good. For just a second, he stopped falling and hung suspended by his foot, but then whatever he'd gotten caught up in let go and he was falling again. He shoved his hands over his head to break his fall, but it was too late. His head hit the hard basement bottom, and everything went black.

Chapter 3
Esther

"So he finally gave you a resume?" Vicky had just stepped into the church's upper room and glared down at the six of them.

"No," Cathy said without looking up. "He gave it to me on Thursday, but this is the first time I've had a chance to get here."

Vicky scowled. "How are you so busy that you couldn't let us know between Thursday and Saturday morning that he'd given you a resume?"

"Sit down, Vicky."

Esther looked at Cathy quickly. That was the rudest tone she'd heard Cathy use in some time. Maybe ever.

It worked, though. Vicky sat down. Cathy handed her a copy of Adam Lattin's application packet.

The founding ladies of New Beginnings Church were gathered to evaluate their first and thus far only pastoral candidate. They hadn't even posted the job opening yet, but Mr. Lattin had shown up at Sunday service and announced that God had told him to apply.

Vicky scanned the first page. "Short resume. Wonder why it took him five days to write it." She seemed to be talking to herself.

"I imagine," Cathy said slowly, "that it took him a few days to gather the letters of reference and the transcript."

Transcript? Esther flipped through the small stack of papers until she saw the official looking spreadsheet. She scanned the grades. Not an A in sight. Many Cs. A few Ds. And one F. In Exegesis. What was exegesis? She had no idea. Maybe that meant it wasn't very important.

"If you'll look at his reference letters," Cathy said, "I think you might be impressed."

The small room was quiet as they read. Esther pulled her sweater tighter around her. It was full on fall now, creeping up on winter, and they hadn't fired up the furnace today. The one space heater in the room wasn't quite keeping up with the drafts seeping in from around the old windows.

Vicky broke the silence. "Can you be a pastor if you flunk out of Bible school?" She had gotten to the transcript.

"He didn't flunk out," Cathy said, her voice even. "He chose to walk away." She took a deep breath. "He says he's eager to get to work and that school was holding him up."

Vicky snickered. "Sounds like something someone would say right before they flunked out of college."

"Stop it, Vicky," Rachel said. "Wait until you hear him talk and you'll understand. This isn't about flunking. He really wants to get going with his ministry—"

"Easy for you to say." Vicky folded her arms across her chest. "*You* got to talk to him for hours on Sunday."

This was true. When Adam Lattin had shown up on Sunday morning and pronounced his mission of becoming their pastor, Cathy had welcomed him warmly to their service and then entirely ignored him for the duration of it. However, afterward, she had beckoned to Esther and Rachel, and they had talked to him well into the afternoon.

Now Esther understood, at least in part, why Vicky was so wound up. They'd left her out of that part of the interview.

"You'll get another chance to talk to him," Rachel said.

"Yes," Cathy chimed in. "I think we should all talk to him. But I thought we might want to look at his application first, without him here, in case there was anything we wanted to discuss."

Vicky shook her head. "I don't need to look at his application. I think he's too young to be our pastor and I think his grades are terrible."

Esther scanned the resume. He'd worked in landscaping before going to college. "I don't think he's that young." She did some mental math. "I put him at twenty-six or twenty-seven."

"Twenty-seven is a baby!" Vicky cried. "And why doesn't a healthy, godly twenty-seven-year-old have a wife and family of his own yet?"

Cathy groaned. "Which is it, Vicky? Is he too young to be a pastor or is he too old to be single? *You* are obviously going to be displeased no matter what, so does anyone else have anything they want to discuss?"

"These letters are amazing," Rachel said. She read snippets aloud, "A man after God's own heart ... servant-hearted ... a good listener ... patient ... good with people of all ages." She looked up. "I say we give him a shot."

Cathy nodded. "Let's interview him again, formally this time, and then yes, I agree. Let's give him a probationary shot."

Vicky's silence surprised Esther, and she looked at her. Vicky was chewing the inside of her cheek.

"Do you think he can preach tomorrow?" Barbara asked. "That would give us an idea of how he'll be behind the pulpit."

"Good idea," Dawn said.

"I'm not sure he'll be able to prepare anything that fast," Cathy said, "but we can certainly invite him to."

Esther thought he probably had a sermon in his pocket for just such an occasion. She didn't say this aloud, though.

"Someone once told me," Vera started, and everyone sat up straighter. Vera didn't talk much, so when she did, they paid attention. "If a pastor ever claims to hear directly from God, then you should run as fast as you can in the opposite direction."

"I hear what you're saying," Cathy said, "but I think that's a dangerous rule to follow. God is the same yesterday, today, and forever. If we say he can't talk to people directly today, then we're saying that we don't believe all the biblical accounts of him talking to people." She looked exhausted.

Esther felt bad for her. "I don't think we should necessarily take him at his word about this calling he heard, but neither should we dismiss his testimony out of hand."

"Then I just have one more question."

Cathy looked relieved. "What's that, Vera?"

Robin Merrill

"What is exegesis?"

Chapter 4
Levi

Water. Levi could hear water running. And why was he so cold? His ankle hurt worse than any pain he'd ever imagined, and yet he could still feel the pain in his head trying to keep up. Where was he?

He cracked his eyes open, and the reality of his situation rushed over him like a suffocating wave.

He had fallen through the floor of a rotten shack. He blinked his eyes the rest of the way open. Why was there so much light? Without picking his head up, he did his best to look around. Daylight was trying to stream in through dirty, cobweb-covered windows. It was bright because it was morning. This fact scared him. He'd been knocked out—that wasn't all that strange—but he'd slept through all the way till morning? Was that even possible? He was lucky he hadn't frozen to death.

He tried to sit up, but his body was having trouble cooperating. He managed to prop himself up on his elbow. He surveyed his surroundings and listened for evidence of life, but there was only the water. Where were

Shane and Kendall? He looked up at the hole he'd fallen through. It was huge. He was surprised Shane—or whoever had been following him—hadn't fallen through too. He glanced around the basement to make sure, and sure enough, he was alone.

"Shane?" he called out, and a million knives stabbed at his brain. He squeezed his eyes shut. "Kendall?" he whispered.

Nothing.

They must have gone to get help.

They would, right? They would go for help? They wouldn't just leave him there. Of course they wouldn't. But what was taking them so long? It was morning now! Had they gotten lost? They'd both been pretty messed up. Maybe they couldn't find their way back to the car. And maybe if they did, maybe Kendall hadn't been able to drive. Maybe they were dead in a ditch somewhere, and no one was ever going to find him.

His phone. He started to reach for his pocket but then remembered that he'd forgotten his phone in Kendall's car. He almost cried out at this realization. What was he going to do? How was he going to get out of here? How badly was he hurt? Could he even move?

A tentative hand crept toward his head. He was afraid of what he'd find there. Relief coursed through him as he felt the egg. No open wound. No blood. Just a giant lump. He closed his eyes, and the pain eased up a little. He probably had a concussion. He opened his eyes again and scanned the basement. Most of it was a mystery, locked in shadows.

The concussion was the least of his problems.

He almost didn't dare look at his ankle, but he forced himself to. Again relieved to see no blood, he was alarmed to see his foot cocked off at an unnatural angle. His ankle was so swollen that it spilled out over his shoe. He leaned forward to get a closer look, and his head swam. Hurriedly he put his hand down on the floor to steady himself and heard a splash. He looked down to see that his legs had been lying in a large dirty puddle. No wonder he was so cold. Why was there a puddle? His eyes followed the water, and he saw it streaming in through a broken window to his left. As he stared at this hole in the wall, he heard water dripping to his right. He turned to look and saw drops splashing on the floor. He looked up to see water falling through the hole he'd fallen through.

He wasn't hearing water running. He was hearing *rain*. He shivered. How cold was it in this basement? Was he in danger from the cold? He didn't know, but now that he was becoming more awake and more aware, he realized he was *very* cold. The water had soaked through his pants to his skin. He looked around. He had to get out of the puddle. It wasn't huge. Shouldn't be hard. He tried to get up on his one good foot, but dizziness washed over him. He reached out to grab something to steady himself, but there was nothing there. He lost his balance and tipped sideways, and without thinking put his bad foot down to stop his fall—pain exploded up his leg, and he tumbled to the floor where he promptly retched. Nothing came up, and he barely had the wherewithal to appreciate this fact.

He lay his head back down on the floor. This impact hurt more than he'd expected, and tears sprang to his closed eyes. He swallowed hard and silently scolded himself. Men didn't cry. He rolled over and looked at his progress. At least he was out of the puddle, but the floor was still wet and cold. He lay there for a minute trying to slow his breathing, trying not to lose his mind.

Searching

When he'd mostly gathered himself, he tried to sit up again. His head was starting to hurt less, but he was terribly thirsty. How funny to be thirsty when there was so much water around. He thought he'd rather die of dehydration than drink that brown stuff on the floor.

He opened his mouth to call out to his friends again but then stopped.

They weren't there.

He didn't know where they'd gone, he didn't know if they were still alive, but he did know they'd left him.

Of course they were still alive. Just because he'd found himself in such a terrible predicament didn't mean everyone he knew had suffered similar fates.

This thought made him think of his mother, and a blade shot through his heart. His mother. She would be *freaking* out right now. She would have come home from work and checked on him in bed, and he wasn't there. This realization hurt almost as bad as his ankle.

Chapter 5
Nora

Nora came through her front door like a woman half asleep. It had been a long night at the nursing home. She corrected her thinking: *residential care home*. They'd changed the name two years prior, but habits die hard. She'd worked there for fifteen years. It didn't matter much what the sign out front said.

She was starving and exhausted, but before she went to the fridge, she started down the trailer's hallway to check on Levi. It was Saturday morning, so he would be sleeping in, which was fine; she just wanted to make sure he was there, all tucked in, safe and sound. She did this every Saturday morning.

She touched the door, and it lazily swung open.

He wasn't there.

She stepped into the room.

The bed was unmade, but that didn't mean anything. Levi's bed never got made unless she made it. She scanned the room. It felt eerily empty. Cold, almost. He hadn't been there in a while. She didn't know how she knew this; she just knew it. No reason to panic, she told herself. He could easily have spent the night being a stupid teenager. Didn't necessarily mean he was in trouble. Yet there was something roiling in her gut.

Something was wrong.

Not necessarily, she tried to tell herself.

Feeling as if her hand belonged to someone else, someone far away, she pulled her phone out of her scrubs' zippered cell phone pocket. He hated it when she called to check up on him, but she didn't care what he hated right now: the sun was up.

His phone rang and rang and then went to voice mail. Her stomach sank. Something was wrong. Really wrong. He never left his phone behind anywhere, which meant he was near it. And if he was near it when she called him this early in the morning, he wouldn't let it ring through. He would either answer it or decline the call to let her know how annoyed he was. He wouldn't let it ring and ring. Unless his ringer was turned off. But why would he do that?

Or maybe he couldn't answer the phone because he was passed out drunk somewhere. She couldn't believe *that* was the answer she was hoping for. She wished Levi didn't drink, but she knew that he did. He'd staggered in some nights smelling of beer and cigarettes. She wished she could stop him from being so reckless, but she didn't know how, just like she hadn't known how to stop his father from the same recklessness.

It was in Levi's genes.

She stood frozen in the hallway, not sure what to do next. She could call his friends, but that would mortify him. Did she care about mortifying him? No, not right now, and she decided to call Shane.

But what was Shane's number?

She had no idea, and without Levi's phone, how could she figure it out? She chewed on her lip. She needed to go to Shane's house. She didn't *want* to do this. She didn't want to drive anywhere. She'd been up all night, and she didn't even know if it was safe to get behind the wheel.

She returned to her purse, found her keys, and went outside to climb back behind the wheel. She looked down with dismay at all the empty coffee cups. She hoped she would find him within the next five minutes and not need coffee, but somehow she knew that wasn't how this was going to go.

First, Shane's house. Then coffee.

She started the car but then had a thought and pulled her phone back out. She opened her social media app, which she usually only

Searching

used to check out what Levi was up to, and went to Levi's profile. It hadn't been updated in days. She sighed. She went to her own profile, where she hadn't posted in months. "If anyone has seen Levi, please message me. It's an emergency." She hit "post" and waited as if answers were going to start popping up like magic.

They didn't.

It was Saturday morning. Anyone who knew Levi was still fast asleep.

She put the phone down and drove across town to Carver Harbor's other trailer park. It took her a second to remember which trailer belonged to Shane, but then she saw his car. Her heart sank even further. She realized then that she'd hoped she wouldn't find him at home. That would mean he and Levi were up to no good *together*. And there was safety in numbers.

She scaled the porch steps and rapped on the door. As expected, no one answered. She knocked again. Still nothing. She turned the doorknob. It was unlocked. She pushed the door open a foot. "Shane?" She'd only met Shane's mother a few times but knew enough to know she didn't want to deal with her right now. "Shane?" she called with more volume. It was dark inside the trailer and smelled of stale marijuana. She pushed the door open the rest of the way and stepped into the darkness. "Shane? It's Nora, Levi's mom. I need to talk to you."

She heard rustling and held her breath, listening.

Someone was coming down the hall. She hoped it was Shane, not his mother.

It was. He wore pajama pants and a ratty T-shirt, and his hair was disheveled. He looked tired, but it was the kind of tired that suggested he was a teenager who hadn't gotten to sleep till noon, not the kind of tired that suggested he hadn't gone to bed the night before.

He stopped in the middle of his cluttered living room.

"Hey, Shane. Have you seen Levi?"

Slowly, he shook his head and looked away from her toward his couch as if someone were sitting there.

Her eyes followed his, but the couch was empty. Had he expected to find Levi there? "Were you with him last night?"

He shook his head again, still staring at the couch.

This wasn't right. If Levi hadn't been with Shane, then who had he been with? She stepped closer. "It's all right, Shane. You

Searching

won't be in trouble if something bad happened." She didn't know if this was true, but he was acting like a kid who had been involved in something bad happening.

He shook his head quickly. "Nothing bad happened." His head jerked back an inch as if he'd said something he hadn't meant to say. "I think Levi was with Kendall last night."

"Kendall? Kendall Cooper?"

Shane nodded eagerly.

"Do you know where they were going? What they were doing?"

"Nah." He was obviously becoming more awake now and had decided to try to act cool.

She hesitated. What question should she ask next? "Do you have Kendall's phone number?"

Still staring at the couch, he shook his head.

This was bull. Why wouldn't he know Kendall's number? "Are you sure? Maybe you could check your phone."

Finally, he looked at her, and his eyes were icy. "I don't know his number, and I don't know where Levi is." He hadn't said the words, but his tone told her to get out of his home.

Instead, she stepped closer. "If anything bad happened to Levi, and you don't help him, you *will* be in trouble."

He flinched, but only a little. "Lady, I don't know where Levi is. Now I'm going back to bed." And then he turned and walked away from her, and Nora had no idea how to make him do anything else.

Chapter 6
Nora

Nora didn't know where Kendall Cooper lived, and thanks to Shane, didn't have a phone number. That kid had been lying. But why? Was he afraid of what Kendall would do if he gave her his phone number? Was Kendall really that bad of a dude? A chill raced through her. If he was, she really didn't want her son hanging out with him.

A wave of guilt rushed over her. This was her fault. She hadn't been paying enough attention. She hadn't been firm enough with Levi when he was little. No. She shook her head. Levi had better sense than that. He wouldn't hang out with a kid that bad, a kid that *dangerous*.

She turned on the windshield wipers. Great. Rain. Just what she needed.

Thanks to the size of Carver Harbor, she did know where a few of Levi's classmates lived. They weren't kids that Levi would hang out with, necessarily, but they might know where Kendall lived.

Which classmate lived the closest to where she was right now?

Jason DeGrave.

At least, he *used* to live close by. His parents had split up, and she didn't know if he still lived in the same house or if he'd left with one of his parents, but she decided to try it anyway. She turned onto his street. Was she really going to do this? Expose herself as an overprotective, overly emotional mom? Would Levi be tortured about this later? She didn't care, she told herself. Served him right for not calling and telling her where he was. She slowed down to turn into Jason's driveway but then saw someone jogging down the street. Was that him? She accelerated, hoping so. Much less weird to pull up alongside him than to knock on his door.

Or was it?

She drove beyond him and then stopped and got out to face him. She shivered and pulled her jacket tighter around her. Wherever Levi was, she hoped he was indoors, warm, and out of the rain.

Yes, that was Jason. Good. "Hey, Jason."

He looked surprised, but he slowed his jog to a walk. "Hey." He pulled an earbud out of his ear and draped the cord behind his neck.

"Sorry to interrupt your exercise ..." She winced at the dorkiness of her own words. "I'm Levi's mom." Doubts overwhelmed her. "Levi *Langford's* mom."

Searching

Jason stopped moving altogether and smiled. "Yes, I recognized you." Rain dripped out of his hair and down his face.

She couldn't believe this child was choosing to run in the rain. Or maybe he'd started before the rain had. "Good. Thank you. Well, he never came home last night, and I'm kind of freaking out." She forced a laugh.

Jason didn't join her in her laugh. He furrowed his brow instead.

His taking this seriously made her feel much better. So maybe she wasn't freaking out over nothing. Words rushed out of her then: "I heard he was with Kendall Cooper, and I would like to go to Kendall's house to check and see if he's home, but I don't know where Kendall lives. I was hoping you might know?"

Jason's frown deepened, and Nora's feeling of foolishness returned. Jason was probably wondering why she'd picked him of all people. Carver Harbor was a small town, but there were still social layers to it, and Jason didn't belong to Levi and Kendall's layer. She cringed at the thought of Levi and Kendall being in the same layer.

"Kendall moves around a lot."

How could someone move around a lot in Carver Harbor? There were only so many places to move. Nora nodded, embarrassed. "Okay, sorry to bother you."

"No, no, hang on. I think I can figure it out." He pulled his phone out of the front pocket of his sweatshirt. He scrolled for a few seconds and then held the phone to his ear. "Hey ... yeah, yeah, yeah"—Nora got the impression he'd woken someone up— "I need an address for Kendall." He rolled his eyes. "Just tell me."

It was clear that whoever was on the other end of the line thought it strange that the likes of Jason DeGrave would be asking for Kendall's address.

"No, no, it's a long story. It's for a friend ... okay, great. Now, was that so hard? I owe you one." He hung up and gave her a small smile. "He's on Canal Street. She didn't know the number, but she said it's the gray one with all the junk cars out front." He frowned. "You want me to go with you?"

"No, no," she said quickly. "Thank you, though."

He nodded. "Let me know if you need any help. There are other people I could call, ask if they've seen him."

His offer stunned her. Why was this young man so pleasant? "Yeah ..." She had trouble finding words. A sense of urgency was pushing in on her from all sides, making it hard to think. "Can I give you my number?"

He nodded, holding his phone up again.

She told him her number and then felt self-conscious. "I'm not trying to make drama. He's not in trouble or anything. If he's safe, then I just want to know it." But she knew that he wasn't safe.

The sober expression on Jason's face suggested he knew the same thing. "I'll make some calls."

"Thank you, Jason."

Chapter 7
Levi

Levi couldn't decide which was his most pressing concern. He was incredibly thirsty. His pants and the bottom of his shirt were soaking wet, and he was very cold. Whether or not this cold was dangerous, he didn't know, but it sure was uncomfortable. He hadn't lost feeling in any part of his body, so he didn't think he was in danger of frostbite or of losing any limbs. It was only November, but it was Maine. He tried to guess the temperature, but without his phone, didn't have a clue. It could be fifty degrees out. It could be twenty. He thought twenty was significantly more dangerous than fifty. He hoped his friends had lived through the night and gone for help, and he hoped that help was on the way.

Because something was throwing a giant dark cloud over both his thirst and his cold, and that something was the pain of his smashed ankle. It shot up through his leg and past his knee. Sometimes he swore he could feel it in his fingertips. He'd managed to drag himself over to the wall and leaned against it. This hadn't increased his comfort any, but it

Searching

had given him more of a sense of control. Now he could see the entire basement, including the rickety, mostly-collapsed stairway.

There was no railing, and most of the steps were missing entirely. A skilled gymnast might be able to climb them, but he sure couldn't, not in his condition. And even if by some miracle he did make it to the top of the steps, the floor all the way around the stairway had caved in.

And would he even be better off on the first floor? Even if he could manage it, then what? It wasn't like he could walk back to the road on that ankle. And he knew he couldn't hop that far. And even if he managed that, even if he somehow managed to climb out of the basement and get to the road, then what? They were in the middle of nowhere. *He*, he corrected himself. *He* was in the middle of nowhere. There was no *they* anymore.

Better to just sit and wait for the ambulance. His mother would be looking for him by now. She would ask Shane, and Shane would tell her where he was.

It occurred to him to pray. He'd never been the religious type, but what did he have to lose? No one would ever know. He closed his eyes and opened his mouth, but no words came. Finally, he managed, "Help me." He said it aloud, but the weakness of his own voice scared him. Why did he sound so feeble? He reevaluated his head wound. Maybe it was worse than he thought. It did hurt an awful lot, and he was dizzy, but both of those feelings were overpowered by the pain in his ankle and the cold. He looked toward the window, where a steady trickle of rain was coming in. That water wasn't brown. If he could get to that water, maybe it would be worth it.

It was a long way away, but what else did he have to do? Might as well have a goal, something to keep him busy. He reached out and put his hand on the cold floor a few feet away from his butt. Why couldn't this basement have a cement floor instead of a dirt one? Wouldn't that make this a less sloppy affair? Then again, hitting his head on cement might have killed him. He put his weight on his hand and tried to drag his butt across the floor.

A bomb of pain went off in his leg, and he cried out at the surprise and power of it. He stopped moving and braced himself for more, but the explosion settled back into the same steady pain he'd felt before he'd started to move. He looked back the way he'd come: he'd moved about three inches.

It wasn't worth it. He'd rather stay thirsty. He leaned his head back against the cool cement wall, and this time, when the tears came, he didn't fight them. They came out of the corners of his eyes and ran down his cold cheeks—and he relished their warmth.

Chapter 8
Nora

Something about Kendall's house made Nora's blood run cold.

This wasn't a good place.

This wasn't a safe place.

Bad things happened here.

She forced her feet out of the car and prayed for the first time in years. *If you get me my son back, I promise to give the rest of my life to you. Please, just let him be alive. I'll do anything.* She raised her hand to knock on the door, but it swung open to reveal a man with a cigarette between his lips.

"C'na help ya?" He leaned heavily on the door frame.

She swallowed, her mouth dry as a bone. "I was hoping to speak to Kendall. Is he home?"

He looked her up and down, and she shifted her weight uncomfortably. "Who's askin'?"

"I'm Nora, Levi's mom?"

The man's face registered no recognition.

"Levi is in Kendall's class. They're friends."

The man looked skeptical, but he stopped leaning on the door frame and stood up straighter.

Searching

Nora was desperate for any encouragement, so she took this as some.

"Are you accusing Kendall of somethin'?"

Okay, maybe not encouraging. "No, no," she said quickly, "not at all. I just need to talk to Levi. Thought maybe Kendall could tell me where he is." She bit her lip, unsure if she'd said too much. "It's kind of an emergency."

The man hesitated and then looked over his shoulder. "Kendall!" he hollered. Then, still facing that way, he waited. When no answer came, he looked at Nora. "Wait here." Then he slammed the door in her face.

She waited for so long that she thought he might not be coming back. She was contemplating knocking again when the door opened, and a young man stood looking at her with cold eyes.

"Good morning," she said, even though it felt like the middle of the night to her. "I need to talk to Levi. Do you know where he is?"

Holding her gaze, Kendall slowly shook his head back and forth.

"Do you know where he was last night?"

Still shaking his head.

"Shane said that you were with him."

He curled his upper lip. "Shane's a liar."

Nora knew this might be true. She also knew something else: Kendall *was* a liar.

"Can't help you." He started to shut the door, but she stuck her foot in the opening, a move that surprised her with its boldness.

Kendall almost snarled. His face looked like a snake's. "Look—"

She didn't let him finish. She leaned closer. "Tell me now what you know, and I *won't* make it my personal mission to see you in legal trouble over this."

Something that could have been doubt flickered across his face but then vanished. "Like I said, I haven't seen him." He slammed the door, and this time she yanked her foot out of the way. She didn't know what else she could say, what else she could ask, what else she could threaten him with. She considered threatening the man instead, but he'd intimidated her, and what were the chances he'd cave if Kendall hadn't? She turned and faced the littered lawn. She wasn't sure what to do next.

The police. It was time to go to the police.

She went back to her car with purpose and slid behind the wheel. She wished she'd gotten Jason's number but then dismissed that wish. He'd said he would call if he learned anything. He hadn't called, so obviously, he hadn't learned anything.

Still wishing she had time to stop for a hot cup of coffee, she drove straight to the very small Carver Harbor Police Department and then parked right in front of the door. She looked up at the nice building with a healthy amount of disdain. Carver Harbor wouldn't be able to afford a police department if it weren't for all the summer people. Not that there were a lot of summer people. There weren't. But those who did show up were *rich*. She made extra money cleaning their summer homes for them before they arrived and then again after they left. She got out of the car and went inside.

A woman behind a counter looked up at her.

"I need some help," Nora said before the woman could speak. "My son is missing."

The woman didn't look surprised. She stood, and Nora read her name tag. Doris. She didn't look familiar. She turned toward a filing cabinet and stood with her back to Nora for so long that Nora almost said something. Trouble was, Nora couldn't think of quite what to say and as she thought about it, Doris turned back toward her with a manila folder in her hand. She set it down on the counter and picked up a pen. "What's your son's name?" She sounded bored.

Nora wasn't pleased. This woman wasn't a police officer. She wanted to deal with a police officer. She answered her question, and Doris's face registered recognition. She knew who Levi was, somehow.

"What was he wearing?"

Nora had no idea. She described his jacket. As she did so, she pulled a school photo out of her wallet, trying not to be embarrassed by the thug-like expression on her son's face, and laid it on the counter beside the paperwork. Doris didn't spare it a glance.

Nora tapped her finger on it, trying to get Doris to look. "This photo was taken only a few months ago." She remembered it clearly. Levi had complained about having to have school pictures taken at all. Nora had rolled quarters to buy the cheapest package available. Buying a package at all was a little silly, as they didn't have anyone to give copies to, but she didn't want the people at school thinking no one loved her son enough to want photos of him.

Doris still didn't look at the photo. "When was the last time you saw him?"

"Yesterday afternoon, before I went to work."

Doris stopped writing.

Nora wished she had lied. He probably hadn't been gone long enough to warrant police concern. Why hadn't she thought of that? "Look, I know my son. He wouldn't take off. He wouldn't not come home. And I know who he was with, and that kid is lying about seeing him."

Doris nodded dismissively. "We'll keep an eye out. Write down your number"—she slid a scrap of paper across the counter— "and we'll call you if we hear anything."

Nora wrote her number down, her hand trembling. This wasn't good enough. "Is there a police officer I could talk to?"

Doris looked annoyed. "Sure. Have a seat." She pointed her chin at the wall behind Nora, and Nora turned to see a line of hard, molded chairs bolted to the floor. Comfy. She sat down and took a deep breath, watching Doris. When was she going to go get the police officer, exactly? Nora checked her phone and then tried calling Levi again. It rang and rang. She looked at Doris. She couldn't see the woman's hands, but she could see her face, and it was pretty clear she wasn't on the phone. Nora stood up again, hoping that would communicate a sense of urgency, but Doris didn't react. Now Nora could see that she was shuffling paperwork around. So she wasn't emailing a police officer either. Nora checked her phone again. One minute had passed. She started to pace, not looking away from Doris for more than a few seconds at a time.

Chapter 9
Esther

"Thanks for coming in so soon," Esther said, trying to sound warm. She didn't know why, but she liked this Adam Lattin. Of course, she had no idea if she was a good judge of character or not.

"Sure. I was just sitting by the phone, waiting for your call."

Vicky's eyebrow arched into a picked point.

Adam laughed. "Just kidding, but I was excited to hear from you." He rubbed his hands together. "I'm eager to get to work."

Vicky put her head in her hands.

Adam's eyes started to drift toward Vicky, and Esther spoke quickly to distract him. "Can you tell us again about the calling you heard?"

Vicky grunted, and Esther wished she'd thought of a different question.

"Sure." Adam leaned back into his chair, looking contemplative. "I wasn't feeling good about Bible college. I'm not saying that it's not for some people. It might well be exactly what many pastors need. But it just wasn't clicking for me. I felt as if I was stuck in a holding pattern—learning how to serve, but never serving. And it felt like I was learning a bunch of stuff I *didn't* need to know in order to serve. I mean, when will I need to have memorized the pronominal suffixes of the Hebrew language?" He laughed but broke off awkwardly when no one joined him.

Esther was confident that none of them knew the meaning of whatever he'd just said. Cathy, maybe, but even that was a stretch.

He took a deep breath. "So anyway, the more I studied the word, the more I was just raring to go. I wanted to *do* something. Not just go to class and study but help people. I want to get down in the ditches and spend face time with God's children. I genuinely love people. I love to be around them. I find them fascinating. In college I was just ... bored? No, it was more than that. I was feeling stagnant, I think. And it was making me depressed." He sucked in another lungful of air and looked around nervously. "Anyway, I was praying, and I asked God for a new beginning. And as I said those words, it seemed they really didn't come from my mouth. I don't know if that makes any sense, but it was like those aren't words I'd normally think or say. And yet, I said them to God, and when I did, something just clicked. Something felt *right.* I said it again, several times, new beginning, new beginning, and then after I

Searching

stopped praying, I couldn't get the words out of my head.

"In the morning, I did a web search, and I found you guys."

"You did?" Dawn cried, amazed.

"I built us a website," Cathy said.

"You did?" Dawn cried again.

Cathy looked annoyed. "I did." Then, to Adam: "Thank you for sharing. I believe you."

He frowned, and Esther wondered if she'd just introduced to him the idea that someone might *not* believe him.

"I believe you too," Esther said, even though she wasn't sure she did. She certainly hoped it was true; otherwise, she was about to hire a pastor who was also a liar.

"You typed new beginning into a search engine, and you found us?" Vicky couldn't have sounded more cynical.

Adam smiled. "You weren't the first result, for sure. I thought it might be stuck in my head because it was a song lyric. So I typed in 'new beginning song lyrics,' and 'new beginning Christian song.' But none of that brought me to anything familiar. I don't know if it was the next thing I did, but at some point I typed in 'new beginning Maine' and that's when I found you guys. And your website made it clear that you were just getting started. And you didn't name a pastor, so I figured you didn't have one yet."

"So God didn't *tell* you anything," Vicky said, and then without giving him a chance to rebut, asked, "Why are your grades so terrible?"

"Vicky!" Rachel scolded, but Adam smiled genuinely.

"It's okay. I'm a terrible student. I'm terrible at tests. I don't have a good memory. I have to read things ten times before I understand them."

The horror on Vicky's face grew and grew.

"But do you know the Bible?" Barbara asked. Then she answered herself, "Of course you do."

"I don't know it anywhere near as well as I should, I'll admit. But I work at it every day, asking God to reveal to me every jot and tittle."

Esther's mind went on a roller coaster ride as he spoke. At first, she was scared that he didn't know the Bible well enough to lead them. Then she thought maybe he was a humble man. She should be more wary of a man who claimed to know the Bible inside and out. But when he said the words "jot and tittle," her mind was put completely at ease. This was the one. This was their pastor. Only

Searching

a man who knew the Bible would use that phrase. Only a man who really wanted to know the word would want to know every jot and tittle.

Vicky opened her mouth to speak.

Esther cut her off. "Mr. Lattin, I'll tell you right up front that I like you and I think you're the man for the job."

He smiled, but managed to look hesitant, as if waiting for the "but."

The "but" came. "But we have a rather unusual vision for this church." Esther looked at Cathy. "Can you explain it?" She knew Cathy could do it better.

Cathy nodded. "We want to really focus on helping—"

He held up a hand. "I don't want to be rude but may I?"

Cathy nodded and swept her arm in a welcome gesture.

He leaned forward and rested his forearms on his knees. His eyes scanned the eyes of his interviewers—all seven of them. He paused to look them each in the eye before saying, "I've seen your stockpiles of food, and I almost wept with joy at the sight. I think that your vision goes something like this. I think you're tired of the churchiness. Of the getting dressed up and gathering together on Sundays to eat doughnuts."

Esther had no plans to give up the doughnut tradition, but she liked where he was going with this, so she didn't interrupt.

"You're tired of the rituals and routines, of the programs and traditions. I'm thinking you ladies have seen a lot in your time and that you want to *do* a lot with the time you have left. I'm thinking you want to be the hands and feet of Jesus. I'm thinking you want to share the good news with people near and far while making sure they are heard, loved, fed, and kept warm." He raised his eyebrows. "Am I close?"

Cathy's grin spread from ear to ear. "You're more than close. That's a bullseye hit."

He returned the grin. "Great. Then let's get started."

Cathy nodded. "We need a few minutes to talk about it."

He held up both hands in deference. "Of course. Sorry. I didn't mean to rush you. As I said, I'm just raring to go." He looked around the room. "Do you want me to step out for a few minutes or actually leave the building?" He laughed awkwardly.

"Just for a few minutes," Esther said before anyone could tell him to leave. "There are doughnuts in the sanctuary." She gave him a playful smile, and his face relaxed.

"Thank you." He turned toward the door. "I do appreciate a good doughnut. Holler when you need me."

Chapter 10
Nora

A uniformed officer carried a large paper cup of coffee through the front door of the police station, and Nora's mouth watered.

She'd been waiting a long time, and Doris continued to ignore her, so she stepped toward the officer to ask him for help, but at the last second, she grew intimidated and stopped.

Be brave, she told herself. He's just a man like any other. But then it was too late. He was already gone. She wanted to smack herself. She didn't have time to be intimidated. The truth was, she was a little scared of the police. They'd come around more than a few times when Levi's father had still been living at home. She winced at the memories: the blinding blue lights filling up the whole neighborhood; the deep male voices hollering into the house, trying to get Brian to come out; the gazillion questions they drilled her with when they couldn't find Brian. The logical part of her brain knew that the police were the good guys, but they hadn't felt like good guys back then. She shook her head to jerk herself back to the present.

Searching

The next time an officer walked in, she promised herself that she would stop him. She would swallow her fear and her pride and grab the man—or woman's—arm. Suddenly, she madly wished for a female cop. Surely, a woman would understand. Then she looked at Doris. Maybe not. She started pacing again, not getting far from the door so that she'd be ready when another officer walked in.

Except that one never did. She paced and paced, got tired and sat down, couldn't sit still, and got up to pace again. She looked at her phone seventy-five times and finally an hour had gone by. Her frustration morphed into anger, and she approached the counter. "Excuse me."

Doris didn't look up.

"Do you know when I might be able to speak to a police officer?"

Still not looking up: "The officer who deals with these issues isn't in right now."

Nora's temperature climbed. "Can you call him? Ask him to come in? Or maybe I could just talk to him over the—"

Doris finally made eye contact so that she could interrupt her more efficiently. "He's busy with something else. I'm not going to bother him right this second."

A lump swelled in Nora's throat. She tried to speak past it, and the squeaky weakness in her voice made her ashamed. "I know my son, and I'm telling you, he's in *trouble*. He needs help. Please. Help me."

Doris's expression softened. She sighed, nodded, and spun toward the phone.

Nora stepped closer to hear, but Doris kept her voice low and didn't say much. When she hung up, she looked at Nora. "He said he'll keep his eyes open."

Nora hesitated, waiting for more, but nothing came. "That's it?"

Doris let out a long breath. "That's it for now. I'm sorry, but we know your son." She looked out the window. "It's morning. He stayed out all night causing trouble, and while you're here worrying, he's probably already home in bed." She tried for a smile. "Why don't you go home and check? If he's not there, I'm sure he will be soon. He'll need to eat and sleep. Call us again tonight if you still haven't seen him." She stopped talking, but then like an afterthought, she tagged on, "But don't worry. Officer Pettiford really will keep his eyes peeled for him."

Nora spent a few seconds staring at her dumbly, trying to think of an argument, but none came. As she turned to go, out of habit she opened her mouth to thank the woman but then decided against it and snapped her mouth shut. Her face was burning, and as she stepped outside, the rain did nothing to cool her.

    She trudged toward her car, trying to calm her breathing. She'd never hyperventilated before and wondered if she was on the verge. She was so exhausted. If she didn't find him soon, she wasn't sure she was going to survive this.

Chapter 11
Nora

Nora knew before she left the police station that Levi wasn't home. She knew it all the way home, and she knew it as she walked into her quiet house and down the hall to his bedroom. Yet, when she saw his still-empty bed, the disappointment was crushing. Maybe she had harbored some hope after all.

Levi's cat sat on his windowsill, looking out at the street. She was waiting for him too.

Nora leaned back against the paneled wall and closed her eyes. Think, Nora, think. How am I going to find him? Her eyes popped open. The phone.

She rushed to the laptop. Their cell service provider had a phone tracking feature in case someone lost their phone. When she'd first heard about it, she'd been creeped out. She didn't want people being able to track her location, though why anyone would need to, she had no idea. She was never anywhere but at home and at work. But now she could see the value of such a creepy feature. She tapped her foot impatiently as their slow internet service brought up the page.

Searching

Finally, there it was, and she chose his phone number from the dropdown menu. A map of the entire country appeared.

Not helpful.

A blue wheel spun and spun on the screen, and she started to doubt that this was going to work. Of course it wouldn't be this easy. A fresh tear slid down her cheek. If this didn't work, what was she going to do? What could she do?

But then there it was. The blue wheel had turned into a blue dot in the middle of nowhere. She had to zoom out on the map to see any roads, but there was one, and then another. He was still in Carver Harbor, thank God, apparently on Clark Cove Road. She zoomed out some more, trying to get her bearings. The name sounded familiar, but where was Clark Cove Road exactly? The map loaded, and her bearings fell into place. She knew where he was. And she knew where he was in relation to her location.

She practically flew to the car. The rain had picked up and it pinged her in the face as she ran. She got behind the wheel dripping wet, again hoping her son was inside somewhere, out of the weather.

She jammed the key into the ignition and cranked it.

Nothing happened.

This was not unusual, and it usually wasn't a big deal, but right now it was unacceptable. She turned the key again. Nothing. She let her head fall to the steering wheel, and a sob burst out of her. The sound didn't sound like it could have come from her. It sounded like someone sitting really close to her had been stabbed. Someone so close they were sitting right in her seat. "Please, God. I'm begging." She turned the key, and the engine sputtered to life.

She sprang up and threw the car into reverse, and then backed out of her driveway with too much speed and too little control. She didn't care. She only cared about one thing right now—the same one thing she'd been prioritizing since he had arrived in her womb.

Once she got a hold of him, she was never letting go again. He was grounded for life. The thought of being able to ground him made her smile. He was going to be okay, she told herself. He was going to come home, and then she could ground him.

She got to the east coast of the peninsula and slowed. She wasn't sure which way to turn. She considered the GPS but decided that would take too long. She turned left.

Her guess proved out. The little green sign that read Clark Cove Road came into view. She stepped on the brake. As she made the turn, her eyes scanned the larger sign that stood on the end of the road. "Private Road" it declared, with small wooden tags hanging from it in neat rows. Each stained tag bore the name of one of the camps or homes on this private road. She hadn't driven down here in ages and didn't know what was down here now. What rich person's camp would he be at? Or had some other kind of building sprung up on this road in recent years?

The summer homes were few and far between, and she slowed as she passed each of them. They all looked deserted with a thick layer of wet leaves on top of tall dead grass. She saw no signs of life. She reached the end of the road, where two mansions sat. She didn't know if they were technically mansions, but they seemed it to her. There were vehicles in each yard. She couldn't imagine a scenario where he would be in one of those sprawling houses. So where was he? Should she go knock on those doors? Or should she go check the empty camps? "Where are you, Levi?" she said aloud, chewing her lip.

How specific was that tracking app? She opened it again and waited for the blue dot to appear. If it was correct, he was nowhere near these mansions. He was farther up the road. Holding the dot in one hand, she headed that way, proceeding at a crawl, watching the dot more than she watched the road in front of her.

It led her to a spot with nothing but clearing on either side. Her heart started racing. Was he lying down in the grass somewhere? She climbed out into the rain. Her keys dinged in the ignition, and this annoyed her unreasonably. She hurriedly slammed the door, straining her eyes, pushing them to see something, anything, that would tell her where her heart was. "Levi?" she called out. She knew she'd been loud, but her voice felt small in the unpopulated area, lost in the sound of the rain. "Levi?" she called again, trying to be louder. She stepped down into the small ditch and then up into the tall grass. Her gut told her he wasn't here. Or was her gut telling her that to protect her? Because if he was here, he was lying on the ground.

She started walking, scanning the ground to either side of her as she went. When she reached the trees, she looked down at her phone and sure enough, she had passed the blue dot. But she hadn't seen anything! Was the blue dot lying to her? Everyone was lying to her this morning. She was soaked through to the skin now. *Please, God. Wherever he is, let him be under cover.*

A thought occurred to her, and she almost slapped herself. Why hadn't she thought of it earlier? She dialed his number and out of habit held the phone to her ear. Realizing this worked against her current task, she dropped the phone to her side and listened.

All she could hear was the rain. Was rain always this loud? A sound she usually found comfort in now made her feel claustrophobic, paranoid. She started walking, still listening. His phone went to voice mail. She hung up and dialed again. She kept walking, annoyed at how loud her Dansko knockoffs were in the grass. She tried to walk more softly. And then she heard it. To her left. She turned and ran.

And even though she was looking as she moved, suddenly the noise was behind her and she spun around so fast she lost her balance and almost fell. The tears returned then. His phone went to voice mail, and her cold fingers hurriedly hung up and redialed. And then she was moving toward the sound again.

And then she was looking down at his phone in the wet grass. A sob shook her chest hard enough to hurt as she bent to pick up the lonely phone. She straightened and slowly spun around, searching her surroundings. "Levi!" she screamed. "Levi! Where are you? Are you here?" She slid the phone into her pocket and waited for an answer, an answer she desperately needed.

But he wasn't there.

Yet his phone was. Which told her something.

She wasn't a detective. She'd never been into reading or watching mysteries, had never felt the urge to solve any crimes—and yet she knew something now, knew it in her bones: Levi wasn't just missing. He hadn't just wandered off or gotten himself into trouble. Someone had done something to him. He'd been the victim of foul play. She hollered at the forest one more time and then turned and headed back to her car.

And then, much faster than she should, she started back toward the police station.

Chapter 12
Esther

Esther was so excited she could hardly sit still. They'd found him. They'd found their pastor. Now they could be a real church. She hadn't known a pressure was there, but when she felt it lift from her shoulders, she didn't miss it.

"I don't think we can offer him the job till we hear him preach," Barbara said. "He could be horrible."

Esther didn't want to hear this. She didn't want her enthusiasm dampened. But did Barbara have a point?

"That's a good point," Cathy said thoughtfully.

Esther sighed.

Cathy continued, "But I like him, and I have a good feeling about him." She chewed on her lower lip, and her friends watched her thinking, waiting for her to lead them. "I think probably he wouldn't have an easy time of getting hired elsewhere, yet I think he might be just what we need." She sat up straight and looked Esther in the eye. "What do you think?"

Esther startled a little, surprised to be asked so directly. "I think I love him."

Everyone laughed, and Esther's cheeks grew warm.

She spoke quickly, trying to redeem herself. "I like his youth. I like his enthusiasm—"

"You *like* his *youth*?" Vicky cried, incredulous. "What does that mean?" She turned her wide eyes to Cathy. "Don't we want someone with maturity and wisdom? Don't we want—"

Esther wasn't done redeeming herself and returned the interruption favor. "Between the seven of us, we have plenty of maturity and wisdom. What we *need* is someone who can raise up Jason and Zoe and Emma and Mary Sue. What we *need* is someone to lead this church when we're all dead."

Several of the women nodded solemnly, but Vicky pursed her lips. "Well, *that* was morbid."

Esther gave up.

"I like him too," Rachel said. "And I think Esther's right. It wouldn't hurt to have a little vim and vigor around here."

Barbara clicked her tongue. "I still think we don't promise him anything until we see him in action tomorrow."

Searching

"I agree," Cathy said. "Don't worry, Barb."

"Speaking of promising," Vicky said, "how are we going to pay this man?"

"You're going to sell your house," Dawn quipped, and everyone laughed.

"I can't sell it," Vicky said with complete seriousness. "Tonya and Emma live there."

"No one has to sell their house," Rachel said. "We have enough tithes and offerings coming in to offer him a small salary." She gave Esther a knowing look. Since Esther's well-to-do friend Walter Rainwater had found Jesus, church finances had stabilized.

"Oh right," Vicky said. "Esther's *boy*friend."

"He's not my boyfriend," Esther said. "We've only been on two dates."

"You've been on a second date with him?" Dawn cried, not even attempting to hide her jealousy.

"Can we get back to discussing Adam?" Esther said, her cheeks burning.

"Here's what I propose," Cathy said. "We invite him to preach tomorrow. Then, at the end of the service, we let the congregation do a little Q and A with him. Then, we invite the congregation to vote yay or nay."

"Why would we need the congregation to vote?" Vicky said. "That's going to be chaos."

"We let them vote because it's *their* church," Cathy said, looking at Vicky. "And it won't be chaos. You underestimate your brothers and sisters." Her eyes scanned the other faces. "Are we all in agreement?"

Everyone nodded except for Vicky, who mumbled, "Fine."

"Great." Cathy got up. "Let's bring him back in."

They watched Cathy leave and then waited with nervous tension until she returned with him in tow. Cathy invited him to sit and then returned to her own seat. "We know it's short notice," Cathy said before he'd even gotten settled, "but we were wondering if you might be able to preach tomorrow."

His face fell. Esther couldn't quite interpret what that meant. "Of course," he said. "I'd be happy to." But he didn't sound quite happy.

"Then we'd like to invite the congregation to stay and get to know you a bit after the service. Then we'll go from there." Cathy leaned over and patted his knee. "I have a good feeling about this," she said, as if trying to comfort him, as if she'd also noticed he wasn't completely thrilled with their request.

He forced a smile. "I do too. A very good feeling." And with these words, he sounded completely sincere.

Chapter 13
Nora

Nora pulled her old car back into the police station lot and hurriedly climbed out.

Doris looked up at the sound of the door opening, and her face fell. Nora could read her mind: *oh, you again.*

"I found his phone," Nora said and was a little embarrassed by the excitement in her voice.

Doris surprised her by looking interested. "What do you mean? Found it where?"

"I found it in the middle of nowhere, in a field."

Doris's expression sobered. She nodded. "I'll let Officer Pettiford know." She turned toward the phone, spoke quietly into the receiver, and then turned back to Nora. "He'll be right here."

Nora had her doubts, but they were unfounded. Officer Pettiford did materialize in the lobby, introduced himself, and offered his hand. She was dismayed to see that he was the officer she'd almost stopped, the one who'd come in carrying a coffee. She accepted his handshake.

"Where did you find the phone exactly?"

She pulled her own phone out of her pocket and reopened the tracking app. As soon as she did, the map swept across the peninsula and showed her Levi's phone was now at the police station. Embarrassed and scared Officer Pettiford would get bored and wander away, she hurried to swipe the map away from the phone's current location and back to Clark Cove Road.

She was grateful that she managed to do this without complications.

He peered down at her phone. "Clark Cove Road. I haven't been down there in a while. What's out there?"

She shook her head quickly. "Not much. Some summer homes, but I found the phone in a field. Across the road from that field was another field. This means that he didn't just wander off. This means something *happened* to him. Someone *put* his phone in that field—"

Officer Pettiford backed up a foot and held up one hand. "Not necessarily, ma'am. He could have dropped it."

This was bull, and she thought he knew it.

"Does he know anyone who lives on that road?"

"I don't think so. And I know he doesn't know anyone who lives in that field."

He nodded solemnly. "Okay. Hang on, let me get an evidence bag." He vanished, and her brain spun to figure out why he would want or need an evidence bag. Then it hit her. The phone! Shoot, but she'd hardly looked at it yet. She woke his phone and typed in his password.

Except it wasn't his password anymore. She nearly growled. She'd forced him to tell her his password, and he wasn't allowed to change it. Yet he had disobeyed her, and now he might suffer because of it. Or had he changed it? Maybe someone else had changed it. Maybe the person who'd thrown it into the field had changed the password. But would Levi tell anyone else his password? Maybe under duress? She didn't know. Shane. Would Shane know his password?

Officer Pettiford returned with a plastic bag. "Have you touched the phone?"

Of course she'd touched it. She was holding it now. She held it up to show him. "Of course. I picked it up off the ground."

He nodded, and she sensed he was trying not to show his disappointment. "That's all right. Without moving your hand, please drop it into the bag. We'll try to find prints on it."

She was an idiot. Why hadn't she thought of that? Why had she gone ahead and smeared her own fingerprints all over the phone? "Sorry," she said meekly. She dropped the phone into the bag. "It's password protected."

"That's all right." He closed the bag. "With your permission, we can get around that."

"Of course. And when you do, can you read his recent text messages? That might tell you something."

He gave her a smirk that suggested that of course, they would think of that.

"Sorry." She suddenly felt so small and so tired that she wasn't sure she was going to make it through the day. Maybe she'd melt into a puddle right there in the police station lobby. Or maybe she'd just vanish entirely. Like smoke.

He held a business card out to her. "I'll call you the second we learn anything."

She took it and avoided his eyes. "Thank you," she mumbled. "What can I do now?"

"You can post his picture on social media. Ask for some shares."

She wanted to kick herself. Why hadn't she thought of that already?

"Other than that, there's not much you can do. Try to get some rest. Maybe pray if you're the praying type." His body turned away, but

Searching

he still looked at her. "We'll find him, Mrs. Langford."

How could he possibly know that? "Thank you, Officer."

"Carl, please."

She nodded and bit her lip. The tears had returned. She turned and walked out of the police station on stiff legs. It wasn't until she was out in the rain that she wondered if she should have contacted a bigger police organization. Wouldn't the State Police have better resources? They had officers, detectives even, with more experience. They had better technology, and she assumed, better forensics. They even had dogs. She almost turned around and asked about calling them in, or maybe even the FBI, but then she realized how much Officer Carl Pettiford wouldn't like that suggestion. If the Carver Harbor Police needed help, they would call it in themselves, right?

Wouldn't they?

She opened her social media app and checked for notifications. Her previous post had garnered a few comments, but nothing helpful. "Will call if I see him" and "Levi, call your mom. Don't be a punk!" and "I'll be praying."

Praying. She'd take whatever help she could get, but she wasn't confident that praying would help much. Then she remembered that her car had started after she'd prayed. Coincidence? Probably.

She spent too much time scrolling through pictures of Levi. She didn't have many, and most of them were old. He didn't like having his picture taken, and she didn't like provoking his wrath. She wanted to find one that wouldn't embarrass him, but finally decided that didn't matter right now. She chose a recent one and posted it with the words: "Missing from Carver Harbor. Please share!" She hit "post" and then before the photo had uploaded, started trying to press "edit." Finally, she was able to edit her post and she added her phone number along with, "Prayers appreciated."

Chapter 14
Levi

Levi fought the tears. He knew this was a little foolish, as there was no one there to witness them. Yet, he felt as though he had started with ten steps between himself and complete, utter hopelessness and that if he succumbed to his tears again, he would be taking that tenth and final step.

So, he held them back. Even though his leg hurt worse than he imagined pain could ever hurt. Even though when he opened his eyes, his head hurt more than his leg. Even though his throat burned with thirst. Even though the pain had already made him dry heave multiple times. Even though he missed his mother and was nearly dying from guilt—he knew the fear he was causing her.

He didn't cry.

"Son."

Levi stopped breathing. The word had been whispered so quietly, he wasn't sure if he'd really heard it.

Then it came again. "Son." The familiar voice sent a warm rush of comfort through Levi's broken body. A tear of relief leaked out through his closed eyelid.

But this was impossible. Though he knew it would hurt, he cracked his eyes open.

And there he was. Daylight from the basement window lit the smiling face of his grandfather, who couldn't possibly be there.

"Gamp?" he tried to say, but his voice was hoarse.

This couldn't be real. His Gamp had died three years ago. He closed his eyes again and lay his head back down on his arm. As if the injuries weren't enough, now he was losing his mind.

Gamp didn't say anything else, but suddenly Levi heard the familiar sound of knife on wood, a sound he hadn't heard in so long, a sound that he hadn't realized he missed. He opened his eyes again and saw his grandfather whittling. Someone who didn't know Gamp wouldn't have known that's what he was doing. So far he was only removing bark from a thick stick. And even if that someone continued to watch Gamp work the wood, that person *still* might not know he was whittling, because Gamp had been especially bad at the art. It had been a family joke. He would spend hours making them trinkets, and they would smile and say thank you and not tell him that they had no idea what these trinkets were supposed to be.

Searching

When Levi was little, Gamp had whittled him a horse. Levi had thought it was a monkey, and, excited to have a wooden monkey, had shared this misidentification. Gamp had only laughed, but boy hadn't his mother been mad at him! This memory of his mother brought a fresh onslaught of grief, and a tearless sob escaped.

"It's all right to cry, son."

Levi lifted his eyes to Gamp's face. He wasn't looking at him, though. He was looking at his hands.

"You're not really here," Levi said softly, mostly just to hear his own voice, mostly just to remind himself he was still in some control of his mind.

Gamp clicked his tongue. "Maybe. Maybe not."

Levi let his eyes drift closed again. He was so tired. Maybe he should try to go to sleep. He wasn't sure sleep was likely with this much pain, but he felt himself drifting … wait. Was it even safe to fall asleep? He was hallucinating, right? He had to be. His dead grandfather wasn't in the basement with him. So yes, he was hallucinating. And what did that mean? Broken ankles didn't make people see things that weren't there.

But broken heads might. With a sinking heart he realized he probably had a concussion. No, *more* than probably. Did concussions make people hallucinate? He didn't know, but he thought he did know that a person with a concussion wasn't supposed to go to sleep. Now he wanted sleep more than anything.

"It's safe to sleep, son. Sleep is good."

Levi opened one eye again. This was good news, if his grandfather was right. But what did his grandfather know? And this wasn't even his grandfather! This was his own messed up brain trying to give him messed up advice.

Gamp finally looked up from his whittling and raised one eyebrow. "Don't believe me?" He held Levi's gaze, waiting for an answer.

"You're not real."

He chuckled. "Maybe. Maybe not."

"Please stop saying that."

He looked hurt. "All right."

"Sorry," Levi said quickly.

"No need to be sorry."

Levi tried to swallow. His throat was *so* dry. He studied the image of his grandfather, who sat on a chunk of firewood.

Gamp leaned forward, resting his forearms on his knees. "Doesn't matter whether I'm

Searching

really here. What matters is that you are. You hang on, son. They're coming for you."

They? Who was they? His first thought was that Kendall and Shane were coming for him, and this brought fear, not hope. "Who? Who's coming?"

Gamp smiled, leaned back, and went back to whittling. *That* was frustrating.

"They're coming. You just need to hang on."

He didn't know if he could. "I don't think I'm in very good shape, Gamp."

Gamp's knife paused, and he looked up again, a small smile on his face. "It's been a while since anyone has called me that. I'd forgotten how much I liked the sound of it." He shook his head and looked down at his hands. He started carving again. "I remember the day you first said it. *Gamp. Gamp!* You were so excited. And ..." He chuckled joyously. "I thought it was only temporary! I thought you'd get to Grandpa eventually, but you didn't want to. You were always so stubborn." He said this like it was a good thing, like it was something he was proud of.

"Stubborn got me here," Levi mentioned.

"Yep." He didn't look up.

Levi wished he hadn't agreed with him so readily. They were quiet for a few minutes, and Levi worried about falling asleep again. Maybe he should fall asleep. Maybe he didn't have a concussion. Or maybe he did have a concussion, but it didn't matter if he fell asleep. He didn't even know if that no-sleep-with-concussion rule was true. He wasn't a doctor. Or a nurse. Or anything. Maybe a nap would do him some good. Yet the idea still scared him. He didn't want to die. He forced his eyes open.

Gamp was still there.

"Are you a ghost?"

Gamp opened his mouth to answer, and Levi was certain he was going to say, "Maybe. Maybe not." But Gamp snapped his mouth shut instead and pointed the tip of his knife at Levi, smiling broadly. "You almost got me there, son!"

"Because if you're a ghost, then it might not be safe for me to sleep."

Gamp frowned. "I don't understand."

This gave Levi pause. If Gamp was a figment of his imagination, then certainly he would understand when Levi said something that didn't make sense. This thought made Levi more tired. Maybe it didn't matter if Gamp was a hallucination or a ghost or anything else. "I am so cold."

Gamp laughed again. "That's 'cause you're all wet."

Levi scowled. "You're not supposed to laugh at me right now!"

He laughed again. "You're in no position to be telling me what to do."

Levi sighed. "I have to go to the bathroom."

"So go."

Levi hesitated. He'd already had to go once, but now ...

Gamp chuckled. "Are you feeling bashful? Go ahead, I won't look."

With great difficulty, Levi turned his body so that he could pee as far away from himself as possible. Still, it felt icky, and he hoped he wouldn't have to do it many more times. He rolled back toward his hallucination.

"Done?"

"All done."

"Good." Gamp leaned forward and studied him. "I think you might have a fever."

Great. Fevers caused hallucinations too. "Am I going to die?" he asked, not liking how small his voice sounded.

"Not anytime soon. I told you. They're coming."

Chapter 15
Nora

Nora walked into her too-cold, too-quiet trailer and shut the door behind her. She dropped her purse and keys on the counter and flicked on the lights. Then she strode across the living room and turned up the heat.

She paused, staring at the thermostat. She heard the furnace kick on, and a wave of horror swept over her. It was cold outside. Cold and wet. Was Levi outside somewhere? And if he was, could he survive this weather? Yes, she decided. Yes, he would because he was smart enough and capable enough to find himself some shelter.

Unless he couldn't. Unless he wasn't in control of his circumstances. Unless he was injured or sick or dead. She shook her head. She couldn't let herself think like that. Her son wasn't dead. If he was, she would be able to feel it, and she couldn't feel anything right now except for fear—so he wasn't dead.

Levi was still alive.

Out there. Somewhere.

She turned away from the wall, and her eyes landed on their laptop. She went to it quickly, opened it, turned it on, and then bounced her leg impatiently as she waited for it to come to life.

Finally, she had a browser, and she searched, "How cold does it have to be to freeze to death?"

"Hypothermia occurs when one is exposed to temperatures of fifty or less and can occur in warmer temps if precipitation or wind is a factor."

Nora's heart lurched. *No.* She grabbed her phone and opened her weather app. It was fifty-two degrees out. But there was definitely rain and wind. *Please, Levi, get yourself inside. Keep yourself dry.* It was above fifty degrees, so he would be all right. But had he been outside last night? And if so, for how long? And how cold had it been last night? She didn't know. How cold would it be tonight? She checked the app again. The rain was supposed to stop, and temperatures would drop to forty. She cried out. No. This wasn't possible. This couldn't be happening. Her baby could not *freeze* to death somewhere alone. She didn't know if he was alone, but she wasn't there to comfort him, so he might as well be.

She shook her head. Positive thoughts. She needed hope not more terror. She checked her social media app. More comments but no sightings.

She went back to the computer and typed, "What todo if your chid is missing." Her panicky fingers made typos, but the Internet translated for her, and a host of results popped up. *Immediately notify local law enforcement.* Check. She'd done that. *Post a picture on social media.* Check. *Don't let anyone touch anything that might be evidence.* She'd blown that one herself. *Look in your immediate area. Older children are often found near home.* She closed the laptop.

That's what she would do. She'd already done some of it, but she could do more. She went to her bedroom and changed into dry, warm clothes. Then she rooted around in her closet until she found her raincoat.

Then she headed back outside and started walking.

Was the rain letting up some, or was that her imagination? No, she thought it was easing up. Which was a good thing. She wanted to tell people to be on the lookout, but no one was outside because of the rain. She went methodically, up one street and down the other, and she went slowly, taking time to peer at each house individually. She looked behind bushes, on porches, in vehicles, and in ditches. She knew that most of this didn't make sense. Levi wouldn't be hiding behind someone's hedge. But she did it anyway, pausing her search only to check her phone every minute.

When she'd traipsed over the entire village of Carver Harbor, most of her body was soaked to the bone. Her torso, kept dry from the raincoat, was wet with sweat. She found this encouraging. It wasn't too cold out, then. She turned to head back the other way, planning to continue her search, but her phone beeped a low battery warning. She swore under her breath and turned toward home. She would go home and charge her phone, try to eat something, and put on some dry clothes—then she would head out again.

Chapter 16
Nora

Nora plugged her phone in and then went to her bedroom to change.

The comfortable dry clothes made her feel even more exhausted, and this exhaustion made her feel guilty. Her baby was missing; she didn't have time to be tired. Wondering how long someone could run on adrenaline alone, she went to the kitchen and opened the fridge.

The idea of eating made her feel nauseous, but she thought maybe eating something would give her some much-needed energy.

She was wrong. She hadn't even finished her toast and yogurt when her eyelids started to drift shut. She nearly spilled the yogurt in her lap before she jerked awake.

She set the yogurt on the table beside her recliner and checked her phone. No useful messages. And it was now late afternoon. Where had the day gone? Was it possible that Levi wasn't going to get home today? Was she really going to have to watch the sun go down knowing he was still out there?

She tipped her head back and wept. She couldn't hold it in anymore. She didn't want to hold it in anymore. She wanted to cry. She needed to cry. So she cried and cried, and those tears paved the way for her to wail. She cried out like she'd never cried before—a primal cry of the utmost agony, and then she did it again. She wailed until her throat hurt, and oddly, this pain in her throat was the first thing to bring her a hint of comfort.

It wasn't much. But it was something. So she screamed again.

Nora screamed herself to sleep.

And when she woke up, the world outside her trailer was dark. She checked her phone. Nothing.

What could she do? There was nothing to do.

Except maybe pray.

She sighed. Yes, it was time to pray. She got up from her chair and went to the bathroom. Then she started a pot of coffee and got a glass of water from the tap. She drank half the glass on her way back to the chair. She sat and tried to concentrate. *God*, she said in her head, *I don't really know how to do this.* Immediately she thought of her father. He would know how to do this. *I'm sorry I haven't really believed in you.* She'd done more than not believe. She'd actively believed that God didn't exist. Because he hadn't stopped her father—a man who believed with all his heart—from suffering and dying.

But I need you to be real right now because I'm desperate. And I will do anything. Seriously. Anything. You can have the rest of my life if you will just bring my baby home, safe and alive. Please, God. I know I don't deserve it, but he does. He's just a kid. He's got his whole life ahead of him—

Does he, though? a foreign voice interrupted. Nora started. What? *Does he have his whole life ahead of him? A life to do what? He's a deadbeat. What's he going to do with this life you're begging to save?*

"That's not true!" she argued aloud. Levi was not a deadbeat. He was a teenager. He had plenty of time to straighten things out. And it wasn't like he was a criminal. Sure, he had gotten into trouble, but he hadn't hurt anyone. He wasn't a bad person. He was just acting out.

His father was a deadbeat.

This wasn't quite true either, but Nora wasn't as confident about defending Levi's father as she was about defending him. "That's not true," she said quietly.

Levi's dead, the voice said, *and now you're better off. No more worrying. No more losing—*

"Stop it!" she screamed and then stopped, concentrating on listening to her quiet trailer.

The voice stopped.

Had it left?

What was that voice?

Was she losing her mind? Had she already lost it?

"God, help me," she prayed aloud. "Get those voices out of my head. Keep me sane until he gets home. Levi needs me to be sane." Saying these words aloud made her feel distinctly insane.

You're not insane, the critical voice said. No, it hadn't left. *You're just grieving. Grieving because your son is dead.*

Nora jumped out of her chair. She had to stop this. She had to get a grip. She looked around her small living space for a lifeline. Her eyes landed on Levi's eighth grade picture, still framed on the wall. He looked so young, so innocent, so fragile. She went to it and touched his cheek, his freckles. He still had those same freckles. She was desperate to see them in person again. Tears started falling again.

You're not going to see those freckles again. Might as well start adjusting to that idea.

She shook her head. "No!" She couldn't be thinking like this. She needed to kick out the bad thoughts. How could she do that? She needed to replace them with good. "Levi is alive," she said aloud. "He's alive somewhere, and he can't get in touch with me, but he is fine. He is healthy. He is not alone. He is not scared." These words emboldened her, and she stood up straighter. This was working. "Levi will be home soon. The police will find him—"

The critic sniggered. *Yeah right. The police aren't even looking.*

Nora closed her eyes and tried to ground herself. *I need something to center on*, she thought. She needed a thought, an idea, an image, *something* to keep herself focused on what was real. She looked back at the photo, but the critic immediately started yammering again.

"Stop it, stop it, stop it!" Nora said, getting louder with each word until she was shouting. This made her feel even crazier. Her eyes swept past the bookshelf and then went back, stopping on the burgundy leather binding.

Her father's Bible. He'd found religion late in life and spent hours and hours with that Bible, but then he'd died, and no one had opened that Bible since.

And now? What sense did it make to open it now?

Yet, part of her wanted to. Something made her think it might give her something to cling to, a little piece of her father, maybe even a little piece of God.

The Bible is a collection of fairy tales, the voice said.

Nora crossed the room. If nothing else, she would take the Bible off the shelf just to spite that stupid voice. She pulled it from its spot and dusted it off. Then she carried it to the kitchen and poured herself a cup of coffee. Just holding the Bible in her hand gave her a small comfort. She carried her coffee back to the recliner, sat down, and opened the Bible.

But then she didn't know what to do next. She knew she didn't want to start at the beginning, but where *did* she want to start?

Too little too late, the critic said.

Nora gripped the Bible tighter. "Where do I go?" she whispered.

She remembered there was a chapter in Psalms that her father had loved. It repeated over and over again how mercy would last forever. But which psalm was that? Suddenly, she was desperate to read it. She grabbed her phone and searched for "mercy psalm." A gazillion results popped up. Apparently there was a lot of mercy in the Bible. She looked up the first one. Nope, that wasn't it. She looked up the second. Nope. Then the third. Still nope.

Maybe she wasn't remembering the psalm correctly. Maybe her memory had changed over time.

And then there it was. Psalm 136. Her father had underlined the entire chapter. She ran her fingers over the pencil markings. Her father. The indentations made it feel like he'd only left her minutes ago.

She could almost hear his voice as she started to read. The first three verses told her to give thanks. She almost laughed, then stopped herself. No, she might not be *feeling* thankful right now, but if she wanted God to help her, shouldn't she do as he asked? So she took a deep breath and softly said, "I do thank you, God. I'm sorry I'm not better at being grateful. But I thank you for Levi. I love him more than all the world. He's such an awesome kid, and I'm so, so grateful you gave him to me." Her voice cracked. "Please, *please* let me keep him." Through teary eyes she continued to read. Over and over, each verse told her that God's mercy lasts forever.

That was what she needed. Mercy. A greater portion of that same mercy she poured out every day for the patients. She needed some of that to come back to her. And she needed it to come to Levi. "Wherever he is right now, God, please soak him through with your mercy. Cover him in it. Let it keep him warm. Let him breathe it into his lungs. Your promised mercy, God. Please, right now, for my son."

The critic had nothing to say to that.

Chapter 17
Levi

When Levi woke up, it was pitch-black in the basement. His eyes shot toward the window, but he could barely make it out. It was dark outside too.

What were the chances they were going to find him in the dark? Not good.

It occurred to him his hallucination of his grandfather might be over, and his chest tightened in panic. He peered in the direction his Gamp had sat but saw nothing.

"How are you feeling?" Gamp asked, and breath rushed out of Levi.

"Horrible." He tried to chuckle. He couldn't believe how relieved he was that his imaginary friend hadn't left him. He tried to push himself up onto an elbow. "My fingers are numb."

"You're too cold. You thirsty?"

Levi hesitated. How had he known that? Oh yeah, because he was inside Levi's head. He could easily know everything Levi knew. "Yeah. Very."

"You might want to get a drink now then, while you still can. The rain's letting up."

Searching

Levi couldn't quite connect those dots. "How am I supposed to get to the rain?"

Levi heard him move. "It's running in from the window. You drag your lazy bum over there and you drink some."

Despite his pain and fear, Levi smiled. It had always annoyed him when his grandfather had insisted he was lazy, but now the memory was a sweet one. "I've missed you. Can't believe how much, actually."

Gamp clicked his tongue, but when he spoke, Levi could hear the smile in his voice. "I tried to tell you. Tried to warn you not to take me for granted."

"I'm sorry," Levi said softly.

"Oh, son, no need to apologize, and I mean that. I hold no grudge against you or against anyone. I am in a state of permanent glory."

Permanent glory? That didn't sound like a thought that would come out of Levi's head. So then what was this hallucination of his? "What are you?"

"Never mind that now. Get some water on your tongue. Go ahead. You can do it."

Levi didn't know if he could. This imaginary friend of his wanted him to drag his butt all the way to the window, and then what? Lick the stone wall? But he was *incredibly* thirsty. So as insane as the idea was, it was also tempting. He pushed himself the rest of the way to a seated position. When he'd first crawled over to this wall, he'd been sitting, but slowly, he'd slithered down to a lying down position again. Now that he was sitting, he immediately felt better. More in control.

"That's a good start."

Levi grunted. "Don't rush me." He reached out with his left hand and pushed his numb fingers into the hard-packed dirt. Then, putting all his weight on that hand, he tried to lift and slide his butt. Pain exploded in his ankle and shot up his leg all the way to his hip. He cried out.

"I know it hurts, son," Gamp said softly, "but the movement will be really good for you. It will warm you up."

Again, probably not something Levi would have thought of. Had the concussion rattled some new part of his brain open? This question alarmed him. Maybe he was going to stay crazy. Maybe he'd be rescued but continue to see dead people like the kid from that movie.

"You're a tenth of the way there."

Levi sighed. "I don't think I can make it." Wouldn't it be easier if the hallucination just brought the water to him? He reached out again and pressed his fingers, which, as a matter of fact, were less numb now, into the dirt again. Again he lifted and slid his butt. Again pain shot up his leg.

He let his butt fall to the ground and tipped his head back. "Seriously. It hurts too much."

"You need to pray."

"Pray?"

"Yes. Pray. Ask the God of the universe to get you to that water. He will do it. His mercy is infinite."

Okay, now Levi was really scared. No way could those words have come from his brain. He didn't even know what mercy was, only that there was a hospital in Portland with that name. He reached out, pushed up, slid, grunted, and asked, "What's mercy again?" as his butt crashed back down. His ankle exploded again, but he thought it hurt less this time.

"Ah, it's a hard thing to define, as most attributes of God are."

Attribute? He didn't know that one either.

"Here's how I think about it, with my limited understanding. It's ... imagine I've done something that has earned me a whooping. And instead, I am gifted with a warm hug and a heaping portion of Indian pudding."

Levi grinned. His grandmother had used to make them Indian pudding. He'd forgotten all about that sweet creamy goodness. Great. Now he wanted Indian pudding.

"With real whipped cream on top."

"Stop it. You're making me hungry." With no enhanced understanding of the meaning of mercy, Levi dragged himself another foot closer to the window.

"Good job, son. You're almost there."

"If the moving doesn't kill me."

"It won't. It's helping you."

Levi knew now that if he reached out, his fingertips would be able to touch the wall, but that didn't mean he'd be able to drink. He reached out, pushed into the floor, and heaved himself toward the wall with more effort than he'd done so far, and even though it hurt mightily, his heart leapt when his shoulder touched the wall. He leaned his head against it. "There," he said, out of breath. "Now what?"

"Now drink that water before it's gone."

Levi felt around on the wall until he located the water. Sure enough. It was there. A steady trickle. Did he really want to lick the wall? He'd never been so thirsty in his life. Yes, yes, he did want to lick the wall. He pressed his lips against the cold stone and let the water trickle into his mouth.

It felt glorious—the more water that ran into his mouth, the more he wanted water. He greedily swallowed it and then prayed for more.

He stopped and pulled away from the wall. He had just prayed. That was weird. He hadn't meant to.

"Better?" Gamp asked.

Levi sighed. "Yes. Much." Then he pushed his mouth to the wall and drank some more.

Chapter 18
Nora

Nora had read Psalm 136 so many times she'd lost count. She remembered now that her father's favorite verse had been 23. God remembered his people in their low estate. If ever there was a low estate, she was in it now.

How she missed her father. He hadn't been a perfect man, but he would know what to say right now. He would know how to make her feel better. She looked down at the psalm. This is what he would say. The words were right in front of her. He would tell her that God's mercy was everywhere and forever, and that Levi was being gifted with it right now.

Wait. The chapter was clear that God's mercy was forever. But was it everywhere as well? Where had she gotten that idea? Certainly not every human was granted mercy every day. She witnessed this every single day in her job. She witnessed the suffering, the *lack* of mercy. So what made her think that this eternal mercy would find its way to Levi?

Searching

What *was* God's mercy? She'd established that he had it, that he had it forever, but did she understand what it even was? She looked at the notes on the bottom of the Bible page, and they sent her to other verses. A *lot* of verses. Apparently the Bible had lots to say about mercy. Did this mean that God had lots of it to give? She hoped so.

She read through them, one by one, trying to understand, but it wasn't easy. Why did the Bible have to be so complicated? Then she got to Psalm 86:5, which wasn't complicated. This verse told her that God gave plenty of mercy to those who call upon him. She stopped reading and cried out to God again. Again she asked him to save her son, but this time she added a new request.

She asked that Levi himself would call upon God, so that he might receive that heavenly mercy. Then she paraphrased the very next verse, "Please, God. Hear my prayer. Please do what I'm begging you to do."

This last prayer gave her some peace, and she closed her eyes to rest in it, half expecting that critic to pipe up again, but it didn't. It had been silenced. Thank God.

Some minutes later Nora opened her eyes in a dark, cold, damp place. She looked around wildly, not knowing where she was. "Hello? Is anyone there?"

"Right here, Mom."

Joy and relief overwhelmed her, and her eyes flooded with tears. "Oh, thank God." She reached both arms out into the darkness. "Where are you?"

"I'm right here."

She couldn't feel anything.

"Where is here?"

"Right here." His voice sounded farther away now. Or was that her imagination?

"I don't know where right here is. Can you come to me?"

"I'm sorry. I can't. Mom, I love you."

"I love you too, honey. Where are you? Can you see anything?" She couldn't see a thing.

"Not right now, no."

Fear swept her joy away so abruptly it was hard to imagine it had ever been there. "Where are we? Where are you?"

He didn't answer.

"Levi? Where are you?"

Still nothing. She started to sob. "Levi?" she cried out louder. "Levi, can you hear me?"

"I'm all right, Mom."

Oh, thank God. "Honey, you need to hang in there. We are looking for you. We're going to find you."

Searching

"I know. Gamp told me."

Gamp? Her heart sank. Gamp was in heaven. What did this mean? Was Levi dead? "Honey?" She was scared to ask the question.

"Yes, Mom?" He sounded young. Younger than he really was. Too young.

"Are you still alive?"

He laughed, and it sounded like the same laugh he'd had yesterday. So he hadn't gotten younger. This was a relief. "Of course I'm still alive. But you need to hurry."

"Okay, I will," she said quickly. "But can you come to me? I can't see you."

He hesitated. "I'm sorry, Mom." He sounded genuinely sorry. "I can't move. It's all my fault."

"No, it's okay. Because God's mercy is forever. You just need to ask for it."

Her phone rang. She ignored it. "Levi?"

No answer.

"Levi? Are you there?"

Still no answer.

The phone kept ringing.

Grudgingly, she opened her eyes to see that daylight was dawning. She picked up her phone. "Hello?"

"Sorry to wake you. This is Carl."

He hadn't needed to identify himself. She'd recognized Officer Pettiford's voice. "That's okay. Did you find him?"

"Not yet, but I wanted to let you know that we found prints on his phone belonging to Shane Defel. We're looking for him now but wanted to ask you about your son's relationship with Shane. We know they went to school together. Did they know each other well?"

"Yes. Shane is Levi's best friend. What do you mean looking for him? Is Shane missing too?"

"We don't think so. He's been seen recently, but we can't find him right now. We have reason to think he's avoiding us."

This wasn't good. "Then you need to find him."

"Yes, ma'am. We will. I'll call you when I know more."

Chapter 19
Levi

"The sun's coming up," Levi observed.

"It always does," Gamp said.

"So I lived through the night, I guess."

"You sure did. How are your hands?"

His hands? They were the least of his problems. "They're fine."

"Are they still numb?"

Levi tried moving them. They were stiff and cold. "Only a little."

"I told you to keep them in your pockets."

Levi managed to chuckle. "Yes, sir."

"How 'bout the rest of you?"

"Not good. Head still hurts. Leg's still broken. Don't suppose you can carry me back to the road?"

It was Gamp's turn to chuckle. With good reason. Hallucinations didn't carry people. And Levi was pretty sure ghosts didn't either. He glanced at the wood in Gamp's hand. He'd been working on it for a while but hadn't made much progress. "What are you making there?" He thought he'd better not guess.

Gamp looked at it curiously, as if he didn't quite know the answer to that question. "I made a mistake, so I started fresh. A clean slate, you know."

When had he had time to go out and find another stick? Oh wait, he had all the time in the world, because time didn't affect him, because he wasn't real.

"And to answer your question, I'm making a dove."

"A dove?" Levi was glad he hadn't tried to guess.

"Yes. A dove. You need the Holy Spirit right now, so I'm making you a dove."

Levi closed his eyes and tipped his head back. He didn't want to talk about religion.

"They're coming for you, but you might hurry them along if you pray."

"Oh yeah?" He didn't open his eyes.

"Yeah. If I were you, I would pray for mercy, so maybe your pain would ease up some. Then I would pray for salvation. And then I would pray for the safety of those coming to get you."

"Who are they?"

Gamp didn't answer, but Levi heard his knife chipping at the wood.

"Okay, I'll pray," Levi said, surprising himself.

"Good."

Searching

But Levi wasn't sure how to pray. Of course, he'd done it before, when he was little, but this was different. This time felt heavier somehow, like he could mess it up.

"What's wrong?"

"Uh ..." He wasn't sure how to phrase the question.

"Spit it out, son."

"If I pray wrong, will it mess up my rescue?"

Gamp hesitated, which made Levi nervous. "I think there's a couple of ways to pray wrong. First, if you treat prayer like a list for Santa Claus, I think that would be wrong. Don't go asking him for a new truck." He chuckled. "And second, I think lying in a prayer would be pretty stupid. Other than that, if you pray with an honest heart, I don't see how you can go wrong."

Levi considered that. He wasn't really good at opening up his heart to anyone, let alone a God he might not even believe in. He looked around the basement and then took a deep breath. What did he have to lose? He squeezed his eyes shut and silently said, *I'm not sure what to say here, but I promise I won't lie.* He paused, trying to think of what to say. *I don't want to die, God. Can you help me not die? I sure could use a break from this pain. Could you make that go away some?*

And could you hurry up the rescue? Amen. Then he remembered. *Oh yeah, and please protect the rescuers. Amen again.* He opened his eyes and looked at Gamp. "There. I did it."

"Good. Now, if you want, whenever you want, do it again."

Levi sighed. "You really believe in all this God stuff, huh?"

Gamp blew on the chunk of wood, which looked nothing like a dove—or a bird of any sort. "Of course I do. I've seen it with my own two eyes, heard it with my own two ears, felt it with my own two hands."

Levi found this information oddly overwhelming and didn't say anything at first. "But if you're dead, aren't you supposed to be in heaven?"

Gamp looked up from his carving and winked at Levi. "You're talking to me right now, aren't ya?"

"Yeah." Sort of.

"Then I guess I'm not dead!" He laughed. "The grave had no victory over me."

Levi tipped his head back. "It hurts so much. The prayer didn't help."

"Maybe. Maybe not. Oops, I forgot I wasn't supposed to say that anymore."

"It hurts. I'm tired. I feel sick. I'm so cold. I'm not sure I can handle religion right now too."

"Good, because I would never try to give you religion."

Levi opened his eyes and looked at his grandfather. The light in the basement was brighter now, and he could see him clear as day, right down to his whiskers. "Huh?"

Gamp winked again. "Son, the God of the universe defines religion as helping orphans and widows. If that's your definition, then sure, religion is a good thing. But I'm guessing that's not what you were thinking of."

"No." Levi tried to organize his thoughts. "I was thinking of a bunch of rules and made up old stories."

"Ah yes. Well, you'll get to all that. But for right now, in this cellar, let's talk about what matters, shall we?"

Levi felt hesitant. "Okay."

"All right. Good. Here's the basics. The God of the universe wants a personal relationship with *you*, Levi Langford. He created you for his pleasure, for his glory, and he wants you now for his pleasure and his glory. I don't know why he let you fall into this cellar, son. I don't know what he's trying to accomplish, but I do know that he's going to use it for good.

And I personally hope that this brings you into a relationship with him because ..." His voice cracked.

Levi waited for him to continue, not sure if he should say something to try to get him going again.

"Son, I wasted most of my life living without God. Now I can look back and see the truth of a lot of that. Now I can look back and see how things might have been if I'd been walking with God all those years." He let out a long breath. "But that's my story. It doesn't have to be yours. You've got an opportunity here to turn things around."

Levi cringed at his words. He liked his life the way it was. He didn't want to turn things around. But at least Gamp wasn't telling him to ask Jesus into his heart because he was going to die soon.

"Penny for your thoughts?"

"I was thinking about heaven and hell."

"You were?"

"Sort of."

Gamp chuckled. "No time like the present, I guess."

"You're telling me that if I die right now from a brain injury, or if I freeze to death, I'm going to go to hell because I haven't been walking with God?"

Searching

Gamp hesitated. "The question itself breaks my heart." He rubbed his hand over his stubbly chin. "The truth is that I don't know. I can't see into your heart. But God can. The Bible tells us that God searches the heart. What he finds there is between you and him."

Unexpectedly, this chilled Levi. He suddenly felt a little less confident in his stance. "Oh."

"Yeah. Oh. Exactly. It's a lot to take in. That's why you should start now, not when you're seventy-two like I was."

Chapter 20
Nora

Nora woke up in her chair with the Bible on her lap. Her cheeks were chapped from her tears. She reached up to touch them as if to make sure her face was still there. She was living in a waking nightmare. She didn't know if she would survive it.

She looked down at the pages on her lap. She had to survive it. She had to survive this so that she could make sure Levi survived it. She checked her phone for messages, but there weren't any. Her social media post was garnering lots of supporting comments and shares, but no useful information.

She had to use the bathroom. How annoying that amid such giant problems she would still have to deal with trivial things like a bladder. She picked up the Bible and went to set it on the chair beside her, still open, as if she were afraid to lose the page. She caught herself doing this and wondered why? She couldn't even remember where she's been reading. Why was she trying to save her place? As she closed the book, she was filled with disgust. She'd spent most of the night reading the Bible and praying, and Levi was still gone. Fat load of good that did.

She went down the hallway, used the bathroom, splashed some cold water on her face, and then as she brushed her teeth, her eyes landed on Levi's toothbrush, and something in her broke.

She dropped her toothbrush in the sink and sank to the floor, sobbing. His toothbrush. He was away from home, and he didn't have his toothbrush. She tipped over and lay her cheek on the cold linoleum. And she cried. One after another, sobs wracked her body with enough force to hurt. But this pain brought her comfort—she deserved to suffer, didn't she? She'd lost her son. She'd done such a bad job of mothering that she'd lost her son. And now she didn't know if he was dead. Would she ever know? She would rather he be dead than suffer this not knowing. No, she corrected herself. That wasn't true. She'd rather suffer every moment for eternity than have her son be dead.

Knocking.

She stopped sobbing and listened.

It came again.

She picked her head up and wiped her face on her sleeve.

Again.

It occurred to her that it might the police, and she hurriedly pulled herself to her feet. As she did so, she caught a glimpse of herself in the mirror—what a fright. She didn't even look like herself. She couldn't answer the door like this. Levi would be so embarrassed. She grabbed a washcloth and quickly washed her face and then tried to gather her hair up into a bun on her way to the door.

She slightly lifted a living room curtain and peeked outside.

It wasn't the police.

It was Jason DeGrave. What was he doing here? Maybe he'd heard something! She hurried to the door and ripped it open.

"Morning," Jason said somberly. "I just wanted to check in, see if you'd heard from Levi?"

Her heart sank. She shook her head, not trusting herself to speak.

Jason nodded. "All right." He looked over his shoulder at the street. "This may seem kind of weird, but would you like to go to my church? I was thinking we could pray for Levi."

She sneered. "Pray for Levi? Yeah. Go ahead. You pray your heads off. I, on the other hand, am going to go looking for him. Again." She slammed the door shut. Then she

Searching

turned and leaned against it. Seconds later she heard Jason walking away and felt guilty. He was a good kid, and he'd been trying to be nice. But that was ridiculous. She didn't have time to go to church. Why hadn't he offered to help instead of offering to pray? Praying wasn't going to do anything. Obviously.

She stood up. She needed to get a move on. It was daylight, and she needed to get back to looking. She grabbed her sneakers and sat to lace them up. Sunlight spilled in through the window, bright as hope. At least the rain had stopped.

For now. She stood and looked out the window. The bare branches of fall were whipping to-and-fro. It was still windy out. It wasn't warm. As she stepped back from the window, she noticed that the Bible on the chair was open again. How had that happened? She'd shut it—she knew she had. She turned and looked at the door. Had the wind blown it open? Probably. She reached down to shut it again and saw that one of the verses on the page had been highlighted.

Her heart ached. Her father. She reached down and touched the yellow. She'd read dozens of verses the night before and hadn't encountered a single one that had been highlighted. Many had been underlined in pencil, but she hadn't seen any yellow. Did this mean something, or had he not been able to find a pencil that day?

She fell to her knees to read the verse that her father had found so exciting, and she saw that he'd written something in the margin beside the verse. Not being able to quite make it out, she rotated the Bible. It looked like "Ready. Daily." Or maybe that was "Read. Daily." Her eyes slid to the verse: And these were more noble than those in Thessalonica, receiving the word with all readiness of mind, daily searching the scriptures if these things were so.

What? What on earth did that mean? Her eyes scanned the chapter, desperate for context. Her tired brain tried to process. This Paul guy went to some Jews and was using the scriptures to reason with them. This surprised her a little, as she didn't think the Bible had anything to do with reason. *Anyway ...* she forced herself to focus. So some believed and joined Paul's little cult, but others got jealous and got a riot going. Sounded about right. Not much about human behavior had changed in the last two thousand years. But Paul and Silas sneaked off to somewhere called Berea. She stopped reading. So what? She looked at her father's

Searching

note again. *Ready. Daily.* She went back to the verse. These people from Berea received the word with readiness of mind and searched the scriptures to see if what Paul was saying was legit. That made sense, but she didn't know why it would be significant to her father. Something stabbed at her heart. How she wished she could just ask him. How much she wished he were here for this crisis. He might not be able to fix it, but he would be able to comfort her.

She grabbed the Bible and turned around so she could sit on the floor. Then she read the verse again. And again. She knew she should get up and go look for her son, but there was something oddly comforting in this small mystery she'd found.

Her father had written, "Ready. Daily."

It hit her like a bolt of electricity. Be ready. Every day. That's what he was saying. Receive God's words daily and then search the scriptures daily. Yes, that was it! That's why he liked this verse. He wanted to be like those people from Berea. Knowing the version of her father who had existed at the end of his life, this made perfect sense.

Her heart sank a little. She'd listened to God for one night and then gotten angry that he hadn't answered. Apparently she was supposed to be doing this every day. She sighed and closed the Bible. She had to go look for Levi, but she didn't put the Bible down. She didn't know why, it didn't feel rational, but she didn't want to let go of it. She grabbed her coat, purse, and keys and then she stepped outside, her right hand tightly clutching the leather-covered book in her hand.

Chapter 21
Esther

It was, without a doubt, the worst sermon Esther had ever heard.

Pastoral candidate Adam Lattin had announced his intention to share the four essentials of worship, but as far as Esther could tell, the train had gone off the tracks on the first essential. Or at least it had skipped onto another track. To support his first point, Adam shared several anecdotes. He would pause after each as if expecting laughter, and a few times, the kind and generous Lauren Puddy had obliged, but his pauses were mostly answered by expectant silences. And Esther wasn't sure how any of the little stories connected to the first essential of worship.

During the second essential, Adam started to sweat profusely. He seemed to sense his sermon wasn't delighting his listeners. And the more he sweat, the more words he skipped, the more times he said uhhh, and the more times he looked down at the notebook in front of him. At one point he started gripping the pulpit with both hands as if he was afraid that he couldn't stand up without it. Zoe, her teenage granddaughter sitting on her right, gave her a worried look.

He skipped the third essential altogether. Walter Rainwater, sitting to Esther's left, snickered into his hand.

By the fourth essential he seemed to have given up, surrendered to the fact that his sermon was a train wreck and that he wasn't going to get the job. This essential went smoother than the rest, but it still didn't make much sense.

He projected no confidence, had no charisma, and left everyone wondering what they'd just sat through. The exact second that he enunciated the final consonant of his last word, Fiona started to play the organ with extra verve, as if she hoped the music would push him away from the pulpit and out the door.

As the music started, Adam looked at Esther and attempted a smile, but there was an apology in his eyes. Esther returned the smile, trying to pack it full of as much meaning as possible: Don't worry. I'm not giving up on you yet.

Cathy went to the front of the room and hollered over the music, "Please stick around for a few minutes if you'd like to ask Pastor Lattin some questions!"

Searching

Esther stood and turned toward the door, expecting to see people flood in that direction, but no one was leaving. She was greatly encouraged by this. When she turned back toward the front, she startled; Barbara was right in her face.

"Why are we still having the question-and-answer time?" She was in a panic.

Why was Barbara asking her? Cathy had announced it! "Why wouldn't we? That was the plan."

Barbara's eyes grew wide. "But we're obviously not going to *hire* this man. Didn't you just listen to that message? It was horrific!"

This was an exaggeration. "He was nervous. We need to extend grace."

"I'll extend grace till I'm blue in the face, but I'm not going to *pay* someone a salary"— Adam started toward them. Esther tried to shush Barbara, and failed—"to babble on like that every week. No wonder he flunked out of—"

"Ladies," Adam interrupted, his cheeks red. "I've just said this to Cathy, and now I'd like to say it to you." He took a deep breath. "I can do better. I'm embarrassed of how nervous I was, and I let it get to me. I'm sorry I wasn't more confident in the Lord and what he's trying to do through me, but I *know* that with his help, I can do better."

Barbara's face relaxed.

Then Adam saw fit to add, "And the preaching portion of the job isn't really my strongest asset," and Barbara's face twisted up into a knot again. "Thank you for your patience." Adam smiled and then headed toward Vicky, and Esther mumbled a prayer for his safety.

"I say we give him another chance," Esther said, but Barbara was too upset to hear her.

"I agree," Walter said, and Esther's heart warmed. "It's hard to judge someone on a single effort."

Barbara left them then, probably to find a more agreeable audience.

"What did you think, Zoe?" Walter asked. He'd really been trying to befriend her lately. His efforts made Esther adore him even more.

Zoe shrugged. "I'm just glad he's not a hundred." She jerked and looked at Esther. "I'm sorry. That wasn't supposed to be as rude as it sounded."

Esther laughed. "It's all right, honey. I'm also glad he's not a hundred."

"Do you guys want a doughnut?" Zoe asked, probably trying to make up for her faux pas.

Searching

"No thank you," Esther said as Walter eagerly said, "Sure! Butternut, if there's any left."

Zoe nodded and headed toward the back.

When the line at the coffee pot dissipated, Cathy called them back to order. Not a single soul had left the building. Zoe returned with two doughnuts and handed one to Walter. It wasn't butternut, but he didn't complain.

"Thanks for staying, everyone. First, I'd like to thank Pastor Lattin for being with us today and for sharing the word. Now this is your chance to get to know him. Who has a question for him?"

Derek's hand shot up in the back pew.

"Yes, Derek?"

Esther braced herself. Derek didn't prioritize conforming to social norms, and Esther feared he was going to say something that would send Adam running for the hills.

"Are you a Patriots fan?" Derek asked.

The sanctuary erupted in laughter. Adam didn't laugh, but his shoulders relaxed, and he smiled. "You all laugh," he said over the fading chuckles, "but that's a serious question, and one I appreciate. Yes, of course I am a Patriots fan."

"Excellent," Derek said. Then he started to hum a song. "Oh, Come All Ye Faithful," Esther thought.

Roderick Puddy raised his hand, and Adam called on him. Cathy looked pleased that he had taken the helm and discreetly slid toward the front pew. "Can you tell us a little bit about your vision for our church?" Roderick asked, raising his voice to be heard above Derek's humming.

Adam took a deep breath. "First, let me say that *I* don't have a vision."

Vicky gasped.

"There's a vision," he added quickly, "but it's not mine. I know that God has given *you all* a vision, and that's why this church is here. My job is to work toward *that* vision, toward God's vision. Now, if you're asking me for my take on *that* vision, I would be honored to share it. I see that you all are motivated to love God. That means that you put him first in everything and that you rely wholly on the word of God to make decisions. And I see that secondly, you are motivated to love others. And I am thrilled beyond words to see that you don't just mean love them with words. I don't see you praying for the homeless on Sunday and then pretending they don't exist for the rest of the week."

Esther fought the urge to sneak a peek at their resident Patriots fan in the back pew. There was no way Adam could know that Derek had no home.

"Instead, I see you all working to listen to people, to feed people, to clothe people, to get a roof over their heads. I see your eagerness to share the Gospel with your hands and feet as well as your lips. And this excites me. I am beyond eager to help you do all this in any and every way that I can."

Zoe leaned toward Esther's ear with powdered sugar on her upper lip. "We should have let him do the Q and A before the sermon."

Chapter 22
Nora

When the first raindrop hit Nora's nose, it almost broke her. No. It couldn't start raining again. She looked at the sky, and it was mostly clear. Only a few dark clouds threatening to bring more assault.

She'd started in the car and had combed every street but not seeing anything useful, had decided that driving around wasn't a very efficient method of searching. So she'd parked and gotten out to go on foot. Now she methodically crept up and down each street, asking every person she saw if they'd seen Levi.

Most people were kind and sympathetic. Some were short and rude. They all said they hadn't seen her son.

When she came to a bench, she took a break to call Carl. He didn't answer, so she called the station.

It took her too long to explain to the woman who answered the phone what she was asking. Why didn't this woman already know Levi's name? Why wasn't this a priority for every person at that station? How many

Searching

missing kids did Carver Harbor have right now?

Finally, the woman put her on hold and then quickly returned to tell her that there were no developments, and they would call her when there were some. Nora asked if they'd found Shane yet, but the woman didn't know and didn't seem inclined to find out.

Nora's tired legs got her off the bench and moving again.

Soon, she'd walked every street in town. Again. She wondered if she should expand her search. Go further, outside of the village. Or maybe start knocking on doors. Maybe it was time to put up flyers? Yes, she decided. That was a good next step. She turned onto Providence Ave to cut back toward her car.

She heard laughter inside an old church and glanced in that direction. She hadn't even realized that people used this old building. Of course, she'd never thought about it one way or the other. The laughter annoyed her. How could people be happy at a time like this?

She kept walking and was almost beyond the church when the door opened, and a few people came out. She turned back to ask if they'd seen Levi.

It was an older woman, a middle-aged woman, and a teenager. The older woman's expression suggested she was sucking on something sour. Nora directed her attention to the middle-aged woman. "Excuse me?"

The woman smiled brightly. "Hi!"

Encouraged by this woman's demeanor, Nora held up her phone. "My son is missing. Have you seen him?"

All three women stepped closer to the phone for a close look.

"I'm sorry. I haven't," the kind woman said.

"Have you called the police?" the older woman asked.

"Of course she has, Vicky." She looked at Nora. "Do you want to come inside and ask the others if they've seen him?"

Nora looked at the church hesitantly. She didn't want to get trapped in there. She had too much to do. But if one of them had seen something, she needed to know. "Sure. Thanks."

Chapter 23
Esther

The formal Q and A had ended, but a dozen people had Adam pinned in the corner, continuing to grill him. Cathy had dismissed the congregation without calling for a vote. Either she'd forgotten, which Esther highly doubted, or she'd thought they needed more discussion first. Either way, the Q and A had gone fabulously, and Esther was greatly encouraged.

The front door opened, and Vicky came back in with a woman Esther hadn't seen before. Esther headed toward them.

"This is ..." Vicky started in a loud voice and then looked at the woman.

"Nora," she said softly. "My name is Nora." She looked nervously at the small crowd, who had fallen silent. "My son is missing. I was wondering if any of you have seen him?"

Most of the people drifted toward her, but Adam broke out of the pack to lead the way. "What's your son's name?"

"Levi. Levi Langford."

"Langford, Langford, Langford," Vicky said, trying to place the name. "Are you Frank Rich's daughter?"

Nora gave her a small smile. "I am."

Vicky nodded. "He was a good man. This town was sorry to lose him."

"Thank you," Nora whispered. Her eyes floated away from Vicky and landed on Jason. She smiled again. "Hi, Jason. I didn't know this was your church."

"Levi's in my class," Jason said to everyone. "He's a good guy."

Nora looked surprised at this.

Adam pulled out a chair. "Have a seat, Nora."

Looking even further surprised, Nora sat. "I really can't stay. I need to get back to looking. I was just wondering if any of you had seen—"

Adam slid another chair over and sat facing her. "Who is organizing the search?" A few dozen people gathered around.

Nora seemed confused by his question. "No one, I guess. It's just me. It's not really organized at all."

Adam nodded. "Do you know that he's still in town?"

Nora shook her head slowly. "No, but I found his phone in a field out on Clark Cove Road." She looked down at her hands. "I think he's still in town. Or close. At least I hope so."

Adam looked up at the congregation. "Does anyone have a Gazetteer?" Several people nodded. His eyes landed on Lauren. "Do you have it with you?"

She nodded. "It's in the truck."

"Great. Do we have a photocopier here?"

At first no one answered. Then Cathy said, "No, but I have one at home."

Adam looked at Cathy. "Do you have a Gazetteer?"

Cathy shook her head apologetically.

Adam looked back at Lauren. "Can you two work together to get blown up photocopies of this peninsula? Get them as big as you can, and make several copies?" He didn't sound bossy, exactly, but his voice carried an authority that impressed Esther.

Lauren looked at her husband. "Can you watch the kids? I'll run Cathy to her house." She swung her coat on and looked at Cathy. "You ready?"

Cathy nodded, and they left.

Adam returned his attention to Nora. "All right. Once we get the maps, we'll chop the area up into sections that volunteers will search. Call everyone you know who might help." He looked up at the others. "If you can help, please help. You might want to go home and get on your walking shoes. And please invite anyone you know who might be willing to help."

Emma looked at her mother. "Can you call our old church?"

Tonya looked skeptical, but she nodded. "I can try."

"I'll get the soccer team," Jason said, pulling his phone out.

Nora started to cry. "Thank you," she said softly.

Adam patted her knee. "That's what we're here for. Would you like some coffee? Or a doughnut?"

Esther flinched. They were out of doughnuts.

She nodded. "That would be great."

Esther grabbed Zoe's sleeve. "Go get more doughnuts. As fast as you can."

Zoe opened her mouth to speak.

"Take my purse," Esther answered her unspoken question.

"I'll go with her," Walter said. "We'll get some other snacks too. And some water."

Adam raised his voice to say, "Can we start a prayer circle?"

"Already on it," Vicky snapped.

Esther looked over to see her and Barbara making a circle out of chairs. This was a relief. Esther couldn't see herself hiking through blueberry fields looking for clues. But she could pray. She could certainly pray. She was

Searching

about to head in that direction when Adam asked Nora, "Where do you think he might be?"

Esther stepped closer to listen to her answer.

Nora shook her head. "I don't know." Tears ran down her cheeks, and Esther hurried to find her a box of tissues. Nora plucked a few out of the box and then gave up and took the whole box, mumbling a thank you.

"I know you don't know," Adam said gently. "But even your guess might be valuable."

She nodded, took a deep breath, and looked up. "I think he was with Shane Defel or Kendall Cooper. Or maybe both of them. I don't know what they were doing, but they usually just drive around drinking. They sometimes go to parties at kids' houses. And in the summer, they drink at the Cove or sometimes in the woods. But I don't think they'd be doing that in November."

"When's the last time you saw him?"

Her voice cracked as she said, "When he went to school on Friday." Her voice was laden with guilt, and Esther's heart broke for her. There was no bigger liar than a good mother's guilt. She silently prayed for God to lift that lie from the woman's heart.

Adam looked at Jason who had just hung up his phone. "Do you know of any parties on Friday?"

Jason shook his head. "I don't."

Adam looked at Zoe, his eyes asking the same question.

"I don't think there was one, at least, not a big one. If there were, Jason would have been invited."

Jason gave her an annoyed look, but he didn't argue.

Adam returned his eyes to Nora. "Does Levi have a car?"

Nora shook her head.

"Do either of the other boys?"

Nora didn't answer.

"Kendall does," Zoe said. "A blue Chevy Cruze."

Adam nodded contemplatively. To Nora he said, "Do you know if anyone has seen either of the other boys?"

"Yes," she said with contempt. "I talked to both of them yesterday morning, but they both denied being with Levi. I think they were lying."

"Where were the boys? Where did you talk to them?"

"I went to their houses," she said bashfully.

"Did you see his car in the yard?" he said quickly, all business. Had he done this sort of thing before?

Nora closed her eyes to think. "Yes, there was a Chevy in the yard."

"Okay, good," Adam said. "And if you didn't notice something wrong with it, then there probably wasn't a car accident."

Nora flinched. Maybe she hadn't thought of that yet.

"So they were probably drinking, and something happened," Adam said. "Something they don't want to tell the cops." He looked at Nora. "You did give the cops these kids' names, right?"

She nodded quickly. "They can't find Shane, they say. But they're not calling him missing or anything. I think he's just hiding from them. Which makes him very suspicious."

"Oh *yes*," Adam said. He looked at Jason. "Can you ask around if anyone's seen Shane?"

And Jason was back on the phone.

Chapter 24
Zoe

Out of nowhere, out of nothing, New Beginnings Church's small group had formed a sort of work force. Zoe couldn't believe how focused everyone was. Even Derek was right there in the thick of it.

While the Puddy kids had helped the new pastor push pews out of the way, Zoe had helped Roderick bring more folding tables up out of the basement, so when Cathy and Lauren returned, they had a place to spread out the maps. Then the new pastor started taping them together—making one big map of the peninsula.

Nora stood looking down at it, still holding the tissue box. "Why didn't I start this twenty-four hours ago?"

"It's okay," Adam said. "We're doing it now, and it will be soon enough."

Zoe wondered how he could possibly know this, but then he glanced over at the people praying in the corner, as if he knew that's where their real power was coming from. Zoe saw that her grandmother had joined the circle. Walter sat beside her, holding her hand. They were so adorable. She couldn't believe her grandmother still had the charm to bring a man to Jesus, but she'd seen it happen.

The new pastor started sending out teams of two and three, and Zoe started to panic. Who was this guy going to send her out into the woods with? Trying to be discreet, she crept closer to Jason.

The pastor handed each team a map with their area highlighted, instructing them to check every inch, no matter how unlikely. Nora had sent Levi's picture to every smartphone in the building, so they could stop at houses and show his picture.

"And remember," the pastor kept saying, "we're not looking only for Levi. We're looking for any clue, anything weird or suspicious or out of place. No observation is not worth sharing."

One might never know it from his sermons, but this pastor's brain was organized, methodical, and motivated. He was brilliant.

But they didn't have enough people. A few of them had drifted off, and very few had drifted in. Tonya sounded embarrassed but not exactly surprised when she shared that no one from her old church was volunteering. Jason also sounded embarrassed, and furious, when he said he didn't know if his soccer teammates were coming. Now he was pacing worriedly by the door.

"There must be someone else we can call," Zoe said, but no one answered her. She didn't have anyone else to call, so she didn't know why she expected other people to.

"I've already posted an open invitation on social media," Adam said. "I'm afraid the weather might keep some folks away."

Zoe didn't think the weather had much to do with it.

"But if you all want to go to my page and share that invite, that might help."

Zoe whipped out her phone and did that, though she didn't know if it would do much good.

A woman who'd been coming to church for only a few weeks took out her phone and then looked at Adam. "What's your name again?"

"Adam Lattin," he said without looking up from the map. "Two Ts. All right, we're ready to send out the next party. Who wants to go?"

Alita came through the door then with Chevon, and Zoe grimaced. Alita bounced over to Jason and kissed him. Zoe looked away and saw that many people were doing the opposite.

Jason subtly pushed Alita away and nodded to Chevon. "Hey, Chevon."

Searching

Chevon gave him a weird look that Zoe couldn't quite decipher. Maybe Chevon was in love with him too. Why not? The more the merrier.

"What are you doing?" Alita asked.

As Jason explained the situation, Alita glared at Zoe—as if she'd kidnapped Levi herself just to have an excuse to spend more time with Jason. Zoe wanted to punch Alita in the kidney. Then spin her around and punch her in the other kidney.

"Want to help?" Jason asked.

"Help with what?" Alita asked.

"To look for Levi," Jason said as if she were stupid.

"Look for him? Where?"

Jason held out his hand for the map. "I don't know yet."

Adam handed him a paper with a section highlighted, and Jason looked down at it. "Wow, that's not that big."

"No, we don't want it to be," Adam said. "That way we can be thorough."

Jason looked up at the Pastor. "But if we're *this* thorough, we'll never get the whole peninsula done."

"We will. We just need more feet."

"Feet?" Alita said. "You're going on foot?"

Zoe glanced at Alita's feet. Strappy sandals. In November. Of course.

Jason apparently thought the same thing because he said, "We can stop at your house so you can change."

"Jason," Alita said under her breath, "you *know* we can't help with this. We have Hannah's birthday party."

"Fine." Jason turned away from her.

"Fine?" she asked, looking for a fight.

"Yeah, fine. Go," he said without looking at her.

"Fine! Be that way!" She grabbed Chevon's sleeve and spun toward the door. "And don't call me later when you want something."

Chevon looked as though she might protest, as if she wanted to help, but then she caved to the pressure of Alita and followed her outside.

Jason stood, jaw clenched, staring at the map until the door shut behind them. Then he looked up and scanned the room. "Zoe. Emma. You guys want to come with me?"

Breath rushed out of Zoe. Thank God. "Yes," she said in unison with Emma. Zoe started toward the door but then remembered Esther and glanced toward the prayer circle.

"It's all right," Cathy said. "I give you her permission."

Zoe thought this was probably good enough. "I didn't know Alita and Chevon were friends," she muttered when she came alongside Jason.

"They weren't last I knew." Jason opened the door for his new partners.

"Wait!" Derek cried out. "You guys should have adult supervision." He started after them. Then he stopped. "Hang on. I have to use the facilities."

Jason let the door swing shut and shoved his hands in his pockets. Zoe had never seen him look so irritated. First the soccer team, then Alita, and now Derek. Poor guy.

The pastor watched Derek walk toward the bathroom. "We need more eyeballs."

"What about other churches?" Cathy said. "I could do a search for a list, and then we could call?"

The pastor nodded. "Great idea. Go for it."

Cathy was leaving her fourth voicemail when Derek returned.

Jason let out a long breath and then opened the door for the girls.

Derek walked through first, singing "Deck the Halls."

Chapter 25
Levi

Levi looked at his grandfather to make sure he was still there. "I think you're wrong."

Gamp shrugged. "Maybe. Maybe not. I've been wrong lots of times. But I've been right lots of times too. With age comes wisdom if you let it."

Levi let his eyes drift shut again. Keeping them open took a lot of energy. "I think I am going to die."

Gamp hesitated. Then, "Well, you are going to die. But not today. Still, since it's coming, we might as well get ready for it."

"What?"

Again he hesitated, this time so long that Levi opened his eyes again to see if he'd left him. "You heard me," Gamp finally said.

"How does a person get ready for death?" As soon as he asked the question, he regretted it. He knew this was going to lead to more religion talk. If he was going to die soon, he didn't want to spend the last hours or minutes of his life talking about religion.

"Don't worry," Gamp said softly. "It's simple."

Searching

No more information came, and Levi was relieved. Good. No religion talk. But then the silence started to gnaw at him. He liked the sound of his grandfather's voice, *needed* the sound of his grandfather's voice, even if it meant they were going to talk about religion.

"How simple?"

"You were born into a broken world, son. Not your fault. But somewhere along the way, you chose to do things your way instead of God's way."

"I didn't even know God's way."

"Yes, you did. You might not have known much about God, but you knew right from wrong, and you sometimes chose wrong."

Levi's chest tightened. "I'm not a bad kid," he said defensively. "I don't hurt people."

"You hurt yourself."

"What? No I don't." Levi spoke the words and then realized how silly they were to say in his current predicament.

"You hurt yourself every time you choose not to follow God. God has good things in store for you. When you don't allow him to give you those things, you hurt yourself."

So this *was* a ghost he was talking to, because Levi knew that this religious gobbledygook couldn't have come from his own head. "So how do I allow him to give me those things?"

He heard Gamp's knife stop. "You say yes."

"Yes? Yes to what?"

"Yes to Jesus. Yes to love. Yes to forgiveness. Yes to life."

Levi was so far from understanding that he couldn't even come up with a question to ask.

They were quiet for several minutes, and the knife started sliding through the wood again.

"Try it, son," Gamp said softly. "Try praying. Try saying yes."

"I'm not going to say yes when I don't know what I'm saying yes to." He'd meant to snap at his grandfather, but his words came out weak.

"No one's going to make you do it. It's totally up to you. But if you do it, you're saying yes to believing. You're saying, yes, I believe the truth. Then you can ask God to help you understand the truth."

For the first time, Gamp's pitch sounded enticing. Either the old man was wearing him down or he'd finally framed it in a way that intrigued Levi. Of course he wanted to understand the truth. Of course he didn't want to believe in lies. But wasn't that what religion mostly was? Lies? Make believe stories? "Of

Searching

course I want to know the truth," he said, and the feebleness of his voice scared him again.

"That's great news, son. The truth is that God created everything you know. He's in control of all of it. He created you. And even though you've sometimes chosen to go your own way, God has made a way for you to return to him, a way to have your slate wiped clean."

Levi groaned. "I told you. I'm not a bad person. I don't need my slate wiped clean."

"Have you ever hurt your mother?" Gamp asked.

Levi didn't answer. Of course he had. Gamp knew that.

"Have you ever done anything to damage the body God gave you?"

Okay. Now Levi wished they hadn't gone down this conversational road.

"Have you ever done anything to hurt a girl?"

"Okay, okay, you've made your point."

Gamp fell quiet again, so quiet that Levi worried he'd hurt his feelings.

"I'm sorry, Gamp. I'm sorry I wasn't always nice or respectful or whatever to you when you were still alive. I really, really loved you, even when I didn't act like it."

Levi heard the smile in Gamp's voice. "I know, son. I knew it then, and I know it even better now. And you are beyond forgiven."

"I was scared when you were sick. Scared of death. Scared that you were dying. I didn't know how to act, how to tell you that I cared." In that second, Levi hated himself more than he ever had. How pathetic. He chuckled dryly. "And now I'm scared of death again, and you're here with me."

"Those who walk with Jesus have no reason to fear death. For them, death is a doorway to paradise."

There was a rustling, and Levi cracked his eyes open to see Gamp coming toward him. At first, he stiffened with trepidation, but then he realized: this was just his Gamp. He didn't know how it was possible, but it was his Gamp.

The old man knelt, tousled Levi's hair, and then pushed something into his hand. "Talk to Jesus. Ask for truth. And then hang on, son. They're coming."

Levi panicked. This was goodbye. "No, please! Don't go."

But he was already gone. Levi didn't need to look around the room to confirm this. He could feel the absence. The old basement was cold, scary, and empty.

With difficulty, Levi brought his hand up to his face to look at the carving. It was a perfect dove. Tears came then. Tears for his fear. Tears for his pain. Tears for his exhaustion. Tears for his Gamp, who had left him again.

Levi was all alone.

Chapter 26
Nora

Nora didn't understand what she was seeing. Who *were* these people? Why did they care so much about her son? She'd hoped people would care, but this level of care was unreal.

Two of the women had called a bunch of churches and then gotten really excited when they reported that some of the churches were sending people, and one of those people knew someone with search and rescue dogs.

Nora panicked. "I don't have any money to pay anyone anything," she said quickly, nearly tripping over her words. "I mean, I would, obviously, if I had it, but I am broke. I don't even have anything to sell to get money."

One of those two women put a hand on her shoulder. "Don't worry. If they charge us, we'll figure out a way to pay them. But I'm betting they won't even charge us. Now they said you should find something of Levi's, an article of clothing or something that the dogs can smell."

Nora nodded. "Right now?"

"I don't know. I don't know how long it will take them to get here or if they'll even show

Searching

up, but yes, let's expect the best and get ready?"

"Good idea, Cathy," Adam said, looking up as the front door opened.

"Hi. I'm Sally, and these are my sons," the woman said. "Put us to work."

Adam thanked them and then handed them a highlighted map.

The woman studied it and then looked at Adam. "That's a pretty small area. You sure you don't want us to do more?"

"We're looking under every blade of grass," Adam said, and Nora didn't feel as foolish about looking under bushes earlier.

"Thank you for coming," she said to the newcomers. Then she looked at Adam. "I'll be right back. I'm going to go get something for the dogs."

"Do you want company?" the woman who was apparently named Cathy asked.

Nora didn't, really, but felt guilty saying so. "Sure."

Cathy followed her outside.

"I came on foot," Nora said, feeling apologetic. "My car is a mile away."

"No problem. I'll give you a lift."

Nora was embarrassed to let this well-put-together church woman see her crooked trailer with the junk in the yard, but it was too late to change course. "I'll be right out," she said before getting out of the car. She didn't want the woman following her inside.

In Levi's bedroom, she couldn't decide what to grab so she grabbed a pair of his shoes, a jacket, and a hat. Then she hurried outside again. When she was back in the car, Cathy asked her if she'd had anything to eat.

"Not lately. But it's okay. I'm not hungry."

"I know, but you need something in your stomach. Got to keep your strength up."

"If I eat, I'm afraid I'll fall asleep."

"Might be the best thing for you." Cathy pulled into the street. "I'm going to buy you a sandwich. You don't have to eat it."

A sandwich actually sounded good, although Nora felt guilty for that thought. Where was Levi? Was he hungry? She didn't argue, though, when Cathy parked in front of the deli, and when she came back outside with a sandwich and a soda, Nora started weeping again. She didn't understand it, but there was something powerful in this offering. Nora could feel love radiating off this woman. Why did she love her? Why did she love her son? Why did she care about any of this? "Thank you," Nora barely managed.

"Don't mention it."

Searching

When they returned to the church, Nora considered eating the sandwich, but then worried people would judge her for eating at a time like this. Still holding her sandwich, she looked at the young pastor. "Can you send me out with a team?"

His expression softened. "I don't think we should."

"Why on earth not?"

"We're going to find your son," he said gently. "And when we do, we'll want to reunite the two of you as fast as possible. I think that will be easier if you're here."

Nora didn't know if this was true, but she accepted it. She felt a touch on her elbow and looked to see Cathy.

"Can you come with me for a second?"

Nora nodded and followed her up a rickety set of stairs that curved back on itself. Was she taking her into the steeple? How bizarre. But they didn't go all the way to the steeple. They stopped in a cozy, square room with comfy chairs along each wall.

"I thought you might want to spend a few minutes away from people," Cathy said gently. "Relax. Maybe snooze if you can. I'll come get you the second we learn anything. Or come back down whenever you want." She swept the room with her arm. "But this is your space. Make yourself at home." She smiled and left Nora alone.

Nora collapsed onto the only couch in the room. What an amazing woman that Cathy was. Somehow she'd known that Nora had needed to eat. Somehow she'd known that Nora didn't want to do it in front of people. Nora started weeping and looked around for tissues. She found a fresh box tucked in the corner of the room. She pulled the tab off the box and pulled out three tissues. When this was all over, she was going to have to replenish this church's tissue supply. This thought made her weep even harder. "Please, God," she whispered. "Let this be over soon."

Then Nora unwrapped her sandwich and took a bite. And it was the most delicious sandwich she'd ever tasted.

Chapter 27
Zoe

"I think we should go to that punk Kendall's house. I bet he knows something." Zoe looked over at Jason, but he didn't return the look. Oh well. At least she had snagged the front seat so she *could* look at him. If Alita had come along, Zoe's long legs would be trapped in the back. She'd offered the front to Derek, but he'd declined. She'd felt a little bad sticking Emma in the back seat with the oddball, but when she'd glanced back, Emma had looked completely comfortable.

"Why are you ignoring me?"

Jason still didn't answer, and Zoe had decided to give up when he spoke. "I'm not sure he would tell us anything."

"Really? The great Jason DeGrave shows up at his door, and he won't tell you anything?"

Jason made a weird snorting noise that would have made her laugh under other circumstances. "That guy doesn't think I'm great at anything. He's hated me since kindergarten."

Zoe blew her bangs out of her face. She was growing out her hair, and it was out of control. "I can't imagine knowing my classmates since kindergarten."

"It has its advantages." He sighed. "Like I know Levi. Even though we're not friends, really, I know he's not a bad guy."

"Then why aren't you friends?" Emma said from the back.

This was the first time the three of them had been in a car together since they'd chased Isabelle across town in the middle of the night. That was a good memory. Zoe smiled. She missed Mary Sue, though. It wasn't quite the same without her. It occurred to her that maybe sometime they should try to get together on purpose. Alita would love that.

"We're not like non-friends," Jason said, sounding too much like Alita. "But we don't travel in the same circles, I guess."

"Circles?" Zoe said. "Isn't Carver Harbor only big enough to have one circle?" She pictured a hula-hoop sized circle.

"No," Jason said, sounding defensive. "My whole life is sports. Levi doesn't play sports. He played basketball in third grade, I think, but nothing since. So I've had no reason to talk to him. Doesn't mean I don't like the guy. Although I am going to wring his neck when we find him."

Searching

"So you think his neck will be wringable?" Zoe wasn't so sure. She worried that something really bad had happened to him.

"I hope it is." Jason finally looked at her. "Why, you don't think it will be?"

She shrugged. "I don't know. How do you get lost for three days?"

"It hasn't been three days. More like two. Friday night, all day Saturday, and part of today."

"That's about how long Jesus was in the tomb," Emma said, "and they count that as three days."

"Good one," Derek said and held his fist out for a fist bump, which Emma readily gave.

What a bunch of weirdos, Zoe thought. "I hope he's alive. We'll keep looking for him like he is alive."

"I hope so too," Jason said. "I hope it'll be just like Jesus, and he'll show up on the third day." He pulled his car onto a dirt road.

"I've never been down here before," Zoe said.

"Not much to see. I can't imagine why he'd be down here, but this is the area Pastor gave us. He's starting everyone out near where she found the phone."

"Pastor? You really think he'll be our pastor?"

"Oh definitely." Jason slowed as they reached the intersection with another dirt road. He pulled his map out. "All right. We've got this chunk of woods right here." He looked out his driver's side window. "I don't think there are any houses on it." He shrugged. "But I don't know." He pointed out the windshield. "There's another dirt road up there, and we've got all the woods up to it." He pointed out his window. "And in this direction, we stop when we get to the brook."

Zoe looked down at her shoes and wished she'd worn boots. Oh well. She'd suffered greater discomforts in her life. She'd also been drunk and lost in the woods before. If Levi was out there somewhere lost or hurt, she wanted to help him, cold feet or not. She opened the car door. "Let's go." Then she had another thought. "Should we split into two groups? It might be faster." As soon as she said the words, she flinched, hoping Jason didn't think she was just trying to get time in the woods alone with him.

"Nah. Safer to stay together," Jason said. "Plus, more eyes on the same area means we won't miss anything."

Emma sighed, a sigh which Zoe thought was one of relief. She probably didn't want to be alone in the woods with Derek.

Derek got out of the car, slammed the door, and swore. "We should have brought orange."

Oh yeah. Zoe hadn't thought of that.

"It's Sunday," Jason said. "It's illegal to hunt on Sunday."

"Sure," Derek said slowly. "And people in Carver Harbor never break the law. Ever." He started to hum a song Zoe recognized. She couldn't quite place it, but lyrics about breaking rocks in the sun floated through her brain. She tried to distance herself from Derek before the tune got stuck in her head.

"Here we go," Jason said. "Let's line up and stay in a line, about ten feet apart or so. Then we'll go at the same speed."

Zoe gave him an inquisitive look.

He shrugged. "That's how they do it on television."

Fair enough.

Jason led them methodically, slowly, carefully in a straight line. Zoe tried to be just as organized and methodical with the way she searched, making sure to focus her eyes on every square inch of her surroundings. After a few minutes, she started to think about Jason, about how much she liked him, about how unfair it was that he was never going to like her back, but then she realized she was doing it and snapped herself out of it. If Levi was out here somewhere, he didn't have time for her angst.

Derek started singing "I'll Be Home for Christmas."

"There's nothing but woods," Emma said, sounding discouraged.

"Yep," Jason said.

"Why would he be in the woods?" Emma stopped walking and looked at the treetops. "I'm not saying we shouldn't be looking out here," she added quickly. "I'm willing to keep doing that, but why would a teenager be hanging out in the woods?"

"She has a point," Jason said.

Did these guys not understand partying? "So he was in the woods somewhere getting high or drunk and hiding from the cops. And he wandered off to take a leak and got lost. Or maybe he drank so much he passed out. Or maybe he overdosed. Or maybe they had an argument, and his friends ditched him, and Levi didn't know where he was or how to get home. Or maybe he's hurt, like he broke his leg or something and can't walk. Or maybe he got a head injury and doesn't remember who he is or where he lives ..." She realized they were all staring at her. "What?"

"You just came up with all that?" Jason asked.

She shrugged. "I've got a good imagination." Never mind that she'd lived through some of that herself. "Or maybe somebody evil grabbed him." She started walking again, hoping they'd follow. "And if that's the case, it's pretty hard to figure out what evil people are going to do, so we have no idea where they would have taken him. Could be the woods. Could be Massachusetts."

Derek groaned. "Oh I hope not. I don't want to go to Massachusetts."

Chapter 28
Levi

Levi didn't know how long he'd spent silently waiting, hoping that his grandfather would reappear. He tried to make it happen with his mind, though a big part of him now knew that Gamp had not been a hallucination. This same part of him knew that it hadn't been a ghost. What it had been, he didn't know.

Please, God, he silently prayed. *Send him back to me.*

Levi had thought he was really scared back when Gamp had been there. Now he knew this wasn't true. That fear had been nothing compared to what he was feeling now. That was a puddle. This was an ocean, and there was no land in sight. The fear made him colder, though his heart was racing. Again he tried to move toward the broken stairs, but he had only gone inches when he realized again that it wasn't going to work. Any movement at all sent a pain up his leg that made him dizzy and nauseous.

A tear slid lazily down his cheek. He couldn't believe he still had enough fluid in him for tears.

Searching

I need to calm down, he told himself. Gamp said they were coming. I need to stay alive until they get here. He tried to imagine who *they* was. The police? The paramedics? He hoped his mom would be with whoever it was. What a good mom he had. If he lived through this, he was never going to take her for granted again. He was going to apologize for everything he'd ever done to hurt her and he was going to spend the rest of his life making it up to her.

But first, he had to stay alive.

He forced himself to take long, deep breaths. He looked out the window. What time was it? It felt as though the light in the basement was getting dimmer. Did that mean it was almost night again, or was it just cloudy?

"At least it's not raining anymore," he said aloud, just so there would be noise. Rain would slow his rescuers down. "Please don't let it rain." He was surprised at how much the sound of his voice encouraged him. He wasn't dead yet.

He should keep talking. But it was beyond crazy to just talk to himself. So he should pray. Right? Just to keep himself talking. "Fine, I'll pray." His voice didn't sound like his, and he tried to clear his throat, but that hurt more than it was worth. He took a long breath. "I don't know if you're real. I don't see how you can be. Nothing about you makes sense, but whatever." He wondered if he'd made God mad. "Sorry. I am in no position to be trying to make you mad." This flippant statement brought his heart a wallop of conviction. "I'm in no position to be trying to make you do anything," he said more softly. He thought about his next words, wanting to get them right. "If you're real, then I have really messed up, huh?"

A new thought occurred to him: did the presence of Gamp prove that God was real? Had God sent Gamp to help him? This sent a rush of hope through him so powerful that his skin tingled. "Okay. Let's say you're real. Then, I am so, so sorry. Sorry I haven't believed in you. Sorry I chose myself over you. Sorry I hurt people. Sorry I hurt myself." He paused, again trying to get the words right. "I do want to know truth. If it's not too late, I'd love it if you'd give it to me." His voice cracked on these words, and he didn't know why. "And of course, I'd love it if you'd get me out of this basement, if you'd let me live another few years, at least ... Please, God. I'm begging you. Don't do this to my mother. Give me a chance to make it up to her. Give me a chance to make it up to you."

Chapter 29
Zoe

Zoe knew the situation was dire, but she couldn't help but enjoy herself. She was with people she liked, doing something kind of fun. *And* this fun activity was also *good*. She was doing something good, something worthwhile, something to help someone, and she thought this might be what was giving her the joy in her heart.

She allowed herself to feel pretty good about herself until she made eye contact with Levi's mother. Then all that good feeling melted and ran away. They'd reentered the church empty-handed. They weren't giving up, of course. They had only come back to get a different map, but still—she felt guilty.

Jason looked down at the map table and whistled. "Man, that's a lot of area to cover."

Adam had lightly shaded the areas they'd already searched, and there were precious few of them.

Adam stood up straight and held out his hand for the map Jason was holding. "Yes, yes, it is. Did you find anything?"

Stupid question, Zoe thought. If they had, they would've mentioned it by now.

Searching

"No, not yet. But we're not stopping. We just came in for another map."

Emma had stepped closer to the table, and her mother had handed her hot chocolate. "What if he moves?"

"What?" Jason asked.

"What if we search an area, say it's empty, but then he moves into it?"

Adam didn't seem surprised by this question. "That's entirely possible, especially if he's trying to make his way home. If we don't find anything on the first sweep we'll go again, and we're keeping an extra close eye on the area right around his home."

Jason looked at the door, which was shut. "Do we have enough people for that?"

Zoe was thinking the same thing. She looked around the sanctuary for her grandmother, who was busy in the prayer circle. "I thought more people were coming?"

Adam's face was expressionless. "I hope more are. Until then, we do our best and let God do the rest."

Zoe wasn't so sure. There were only a couple dozen of them. How could they search the whole peninsula before dark?

"All right," Jason said. "We'd better get to it, then." He turned toward the door. Emma followed, and her mother shoved more food at her as she went by. Derek was over by the doughnut boxes. "You coming, Derek?"

Derek grabbed a stack of doughnuts and nodded. Then he followed them outside.

Once they were inside the car, Zoe asked, "What area did we get this time?" as she snapped her seatbelt into place.

"Right beside the last one," Jason said. "Only on the shore. It was a waste of time to drive to the church and back. He should've given us a stack of maps."

"Nah," Derek said. "The break gave us a chance to warm up our tootsies."

Jason didn't even crack a smile.

Zoe waited until they got out of the car at their next stop before quietly asking, "Are you okay?"

He gave a slight shake of the head. "Yeah. I'm fine."

She wasn't buying that, and he must have sensed it, because he added, "I'm just starting to think we're not going to find him. Or if we do find him, it will be too late."

"We only just started looking."

"I know, but there's a lot of area, and there are so few of us. And who's to say that he's even anywhere near Carver Harbor anymore? He could have gone to Bangor or Ellsworth or somewhere even further. How would we know?"

Zoe thought about it. "The police must have tracked his phone, right? And if he'd left the area, they would have told his mother."

Derek was walking toward them now. "You're making an awful lot of assumptions there, Chloe."

She scowled. "*Zoe*."

He smiled. "I wouldn't bet that the police have done any of that stuff."

Zoe didn't like being told she was wrong. "Hang on." She pulled her phone out. "I'll call my grandmother."

Chapter 30
Esther

"Esther!" Rachel called across the sanctuary. "Your phone is ringing!"

Esther looked up to gauge who was closer, she or Rachel. Rachel was already on her way to the phone, so Esther let her get it.

"It's Zoe!"

"Answer it." As if Rachel needed to be told.

"Hi, Zoe. It's Rachel ... oh ... I don't know ... that's a good question. Hang on." She readily handed the phone off to Esther. "She's asking hard questions."

"Hello?"

"Hi, Gramma. We were just thinking, and we wanted to confirm that the police have tracked his phone, so that we know that he didn't leave the area."

"Oh. I have no idea. I would assume so?" She scanned the sanctuary for someone smarter than her. Nora made eye contact with her, so she headed that way. "The kids just wanted to check to make sure that the police tracked your son's phone."

"I already found his phone," she said tiredly.

Searching

"No," Zoe said. "Gramma, can you put me on speaker?"

"Hang on." It took too long, but she managed to do that. "All right. You're on speaker phone."

"Hi, Mrs. ..."

"Langford," Esther quickly said.

"Langford," Zoe repeated, sounding annoyed. "I'm sure the police have already done this, but I just wanted to check now that I've thought of it. They did track his phone movements over the last few days? Just to make sure he didn't leave the area on Friday night?"

"But his phone was found here," Nora said, obviously confused.

"Right," Zoe said and then didn't say anything else.

Esther understood her hesitation. Zoe didn't want to say that the phone could have made its way back to Carver Harbor without Levi. "Wouldn't hurt to check?" she said to Nora.

Nora's head fell. "I don't really want to deal with the police right now. If they haven't done that, then me calling them isn't going to get them to do it."

"I'll call," Esther said before she thought about what she was volunteering for. "I'll call you back, Zoe." She hung up and started to dial, but then she wasn't sure what numbers to press. She looked at Nora. "Have you been working with a particular detective?"

Nora nodded and pulled a card out of her pocket. She offered it to Esther. "He's not a detective, I don't think, but here he is."

Esther dialed the number, her belly a swarm of nerves. She wished Walter hadn't left the prayer circle to join one of the search teams. He'd be much better at this than she was. He loved talking on the phone.

"Hello?"

"Hello ..." Esther looked at the card. "Is this Officer Pettiford?"

"It is."

"Great. My name is Esther, and I'm calling from New Beginnings Church. We've set up a sort of search party for Levi, and we wanted to check ..." She searched for the right words.

"You set up a search party?"

"Yes. Just a few of us, though anyone is welcome to help."

"Where are you looking?"

"Well, that's just it. We're combing the whole peninsula, but we wanted to make sure that you guys tracked his phone locations for the last few days." She worried she wasn't being clear. "You know, so that we would

Searching

know if we needed to look further away, if he did go further away." She cringed. Why had she volunteered to do this? She should have made Cathy do it. She looked at Cathy, who was still busy calling every church in the state asking for help.

Officer Pettiford chuckled dryly. "You cannot track a phone unless the owner makes calls, which he did not." He sounded beyond irritated.

"Oh." She tried not to let her disappointment show on her face, for Nora's sake. "So does that mean we don't know for sure that he didn't leave the peninsula?"

"We don't know anything for sure. Now if you don't mind, I've got to go—"

"Yes, yes, of course. Thank you for your help." Esther hung up the phone and looked at Nora, who was paler than she'd been a few minutes ago.

"I should have called him," she said and then she let out a wail unlike any wail Esther had ever heard before.

Esther went to her quickly and wrapped her arms around the small, trembling woman and squeezed. The woman sobbed, and Esther didn't know what to say, so she just held her. *Please, Father. I'm begging you. Let us find this child.*

Chapter 31
Zoe

Zoe hung up the phone.

"What?" Jason prodded.

Zoe shook her head and shoved her phone into her back pocket. "The police say he didn't use his phone while he was missing, so they can't track it."

"I don't see how that can be true with today's technology," Derek said.

"He hasn't used his phone since Friday?" Jason asked, sounding alarmed.

"I guess not," Zoe said.

"Why, Jason?" Emma asked. "Why is that bad?"

Jason hesitated to answer, but Zoe gave him time. She wanted to know the answer to that question too. Finally, Jason leveled a sober gaze at her. "Think about it. What kid our age doesn't use their phone for three days? That means that whatever happened to him, it must have happened on Friday."

Zoe had already assumed that, but she didn't say so.

Jason shook his head. "I'm just scared for him is all. Friday was a long time ago."

Searching

"The best thing to do for fear," Derek said, "is to move your feet."

Wow, Zoe thought. That was a fairly profound thing to say.

But as he walked away, Derek added, "Move your feet, lose your seat," and Zoe was no longer impressed.

They formed their line again and started walking.

"This time we go from this intersection back to the brook, and we go all the way to the water."

"How far is that?" Emma sounded tired.

"I don't know," Jason said, sounding less worried now that he was moving again. So Derek had been right. "But it's not too far."

Slowly they combed the woods, not seeing anything unusual or out of place. They reached the brook, looked in it, and then turned and headed back in the direction they'd come.

"Oh no," Derek said.

"What?" Jason asked. "What do you see?"

"I don't see anything. But it's starting to rain."

Zoe looked up. There was no cloud overhead and certainly no rain.

"Okay," Jason said dismissively.

But just as they reached the road again, Zoe felt the first drops hit her head.

Zoe expected one or more of them to talk about heading back to the church if it was going to rain, especially since they could see Jason's car from where they stood. But no one mentioned stopping or leaving. They all just turned around and headed back into the woods, back toward the brook.

The rain fell harder, and Zoe got colder. She tried not to think about it, told herself that Levi, wherever he was, was probably pretty cold too. But when she saw that Emma's lips were blue, she spoke up. "Jason, I think maybe we should take a break."

Emma caught her looking at her. "No. I'm okay. We're more than halfway done with this area."

Jason gave Emma a long look. "Are you sure? There's no shame in going to change into dry clothes."

"We'll just get wet again. Come on." Emma starting walking again.

Jason took off his soaking wet coat and hurried after her. He draped it over Emma's shoulders. "Zip it up. And stay in line. We don't want to freeze to death and miss something."

Searching

Emma gave him an exaggerated salute. "Yes, sir!"

Zoe wasn't so sure. "If you get too cold, you have to admit it, Emma."

Emma gave her a dirty look. "You're the one wearing shoes with holes in them."

Jason snickered. "Excellent point. All right. Let's try to finish this chunk, and then we'll go get dry."

And so they continued. Zoe wondered if they might not be so committed if they weren't together. She thought she'd probably give in to the cold if Jason and Emma weren't watching. And she wondered if Jason and Emma were in similar positions. Derek was different, though. He didn't even seem to mind being cold. He was so focused on searching. She should follow suit, she thought, and narrowed her eyes. It was harder to see through the rain. *God, please don't let us get close to him without seeing him. If he can see us or hear us, please give him a way to get our attention.* This small prayer made her feel much more confident in their efforts. She even felt a little warmer.

Chapter 32
Nora

Nora feared she was on the edge of a real, bona fide, white-van-come-and-take-her-away breakdown, and she didn't know how to stop it. She'd tried sitting in the prayer circle but had gone stir crazy. She'd tried pacing around the sanctuary, but she'd nearly dropped from exhaustion.

Now she sat with one elbow on the map table, weeping quietly. The map was so big, and so little of it had been shaded in.

She was having trouble maintaining hope. Maybe her son was really gone. Maybe he was gone for good. Maybe she'd never find out what had happened to him.

And she knew that she wouldn't be able to survive this. She didn't know if she could survive the next five minutes.

She fluctuated between not being able to draw breath and breathing so fast she got dizzy—sometimes in the space of a single minute.

"Is there anything I can do for you?" a soft voice asked.

Nora looked up to see one of the church ladies standing over her shoulder. It was the

Searching

one who'd called the police for her, the one who'd hugged her. Esther. "Not that I can think of."

Esther rested a hand on her shoulder. "You let me know if you think of anything. I know there's really nothing to be done except find your son, but if there's anything, no matter how small or silly, that you can think of, that would help you hold on until then, you let me know."

Nora nodded.

Esther hesitated. "You want to go for a walk?"

Nora wiped her eyes on her free shoulder. "The pastor told me not to leave."

"We won't. Besides, it's raining out again."

Oh *no*. Nora hadn't known that. Her chest tightened.

"I meant around the sanctuary." Esther shrugged. "I don't know if it'll help, but moving a little, getting my blood flowing usually helps me."

Nora nodded and stood up because she didn't know what else to do. Sitting there crying certainly wasn't helping. She matched Esther's pace, and slowly, they walked toward the front of the large room. "It's a beautiful church," Nora said to fill the silence.

"It sure is. We are beyond grateful."

Nora couldn't think of anything else to say. They walked the length of the front wall and then turned and headed down the side of the room, past the prayer circle. She couldn't believe how long these women had been praying. Then they were at the back wall, where the door was, and Nora stared at it again, willing her boy to walk through it alive and well.

"We are going to find him," Esther said, sounding confident.

"How can you be so sure of that?"

At first Esther didn't answer. Then she said, "We've asked God to bring Levi home. That's what God does. He brings his children home."

Part of Nora wanted to roll her eyes at these words. Another part of her clung to them for dear life.

"I've got a peace about it. God hasn't told me in words or anything." Esther chuckled. "But I've got a supernatural peace about the situation. I think God brought you here, to our church, so that we could find your boy for you." She shrugged again. "I can't explain it, but then again, I can't explain anything God does."

Nora was tired of walking. "I feel like I'm in danger of losing my mind. Like really. Like having a break with reality." She'd seen this

Searching

happen multiple times in the home where she worked. She knew it was something to fear.

Esther stopped walking and turned to face her. She took both of Nora's hands into her own, which were soft and warm. "I want to ask you something, but I'm not very good with words, so bear with me."

Nora thought she'd been fairly good with words so far, better than Nora ever managed. She nodded.

"I ask you this because I'm trying to help, not because I'm trying to judge you. I won't. I won't judge you either way. I'm just trying to figure out how best to help you."

Nora nodded again.

"Where are you at with God?"

Nora managed to smile through her tears. The question hadn't felt judgy at all, and she was grateful. She collapsed into a pew, and Esther sat beside her, turning her body to face her.

"I don't know where I'm at. I guess I believe in him. My dad was a strong believer at the end of his life." She shrugged and studied her hands. "I don't know. I was reading his Bible last night. I read for most of the night actually. I read about mercy. And I prayed a lot." She looked up at Esther. "And so far, I don't see how that's done much good."

Esther's eyes widened. "Are you kidding? That prayer and study brought you here. It brought you to people who are helping."

Nora looked at the door. "Not enough."

"I know. It seems there's never enough help, but there will be. There will be enough."

Nora didn't know how this woman could be so sure about anything. Maybe she was delusional. She did look pretty old.

"Can I ask you how you felt last night, while you were reading the Bible?"

Nora thought about it. "Terrified. Confused."

"That's how you felt because your son was missing. But how did the *Bible* make you feel?"

Nora didn't know how to answer that. "Better, I guess. A little. It gave me something to do."

Esther smiled. "Do you want me to find you a Bible? Maybe reading a little now might help. Or maybe just holding one in your hands. No matter what the question is, the answer is between those covers."

Nora studied Esther. "My dad used to say that."

Esther patted her on the back. "Your dad wasn't wrong." She stood. "Let me go find you a Bible."

Searching

"No, it's okay. I've got my dad's Bible in the car." She stood too and then she remembered. "Shoot. My car is a long way away."

"Let's go get it. Let's go get your car. You're going to need it when Levi gets here. And then you'll have your father's Bible too."

Chapter 33
Esther

"Zoe!" Esther cried when the kids and Derek returned.

"Emma!" Tonya cried, right behind Esther as they hurried to the door.

Esther looked around madly for something to wrap around the kids, but there was nothing in sight. "We need to get you next door to change." Esther tried to spin Zoe around.

"You too, kiddo. Let's go home and change," Tonya said.

"No way!" Emma said. "That will take forever!" This was an exaggeration. It wouldn't take *forever*, but they did live outside of town so it would take longer than walking next door. "I'll borrow some of Zoe's clothes."

Zoe snickered. "Are you insane?"

Emma looked at her, her eyes wide. "What? No, I'm not insane. I'll roll the legs up."

Esther wasn't sure it this was a good plan. Zoe was nearly two feet taller than Emma. "I'd offer my clothes, Emma, but I don't have enough belts."

Zoe sighed. "Come on. I've got some sweats that might stay on your tiny little body."

"Great!" Emma slid out of her mother's grasp.

"Fine. I'll make more hot chocolate." Tonya turned back toward the kitchenette in the back of the sanctuary.

Emma looked at Jason. "What are you doing?"

"I'm going to go change."

"But you'll come back for us?"

Esther was impressed with how seriously she was taking this.

"Of course."

"And you won't start another section without us?"

Jason gave her an incredulous look. "Of course not." He looked at Derek and tentatively asked, "Do you have any other clothes, Derek?"

Derek had just taken a bite of a doughnut, so he answered through a mouth full of sugar, "Don't worry about me. I'll be ready when you get back."

"All right. I'll be right back." And Jason was out through the door.

"Come on, girls. Let's get you dry." She ushered them out the door and across the lawn. By the time they'd reached her building, she was soaked too. She ducked into the warm foyer. "So we'll change our clothes, but

I'm not sure we can get back to the church without getting soaked again." She didn't want to stop these kids from searching, but it occurred to her that this might be the prudent thing to do, just until the rain let up.

"I've got a raincoat." Zoe stepped into the elevator. "Do you have one that Emma could borrow?"

Yes, she did. Emma would swim in it, but she had one. "Sure. And I have an umbrella too." She stepped into the elevator and pressed her floor's button. "Too bad I didn't have a dozen of them."

The girls changed in record time, and Emma came out of the bathroom looking absolutely ridiculous. She had Zoe's sweatpants cinched up around her armpits, and Zoe's sweatshirt nearly reached her knees. "I am *so* warm," Emma said, sounding so happy to be out of her wet clothes. "And you can't even tell I'm not wearing a bra." She giggled mischievously.

Esther still hadn't located her raincoat. "Give me just a second, girls." She rifled through her closet, looking for the old standby, and in the process, stumbled onto an incredibly ugly yellow rain hat. No way would Zoe be caught dead in such a thing—under normal circumstances. She finally found the raincoat and then she carried both finds out into the living room. "Here's a coat for you, Emma, and do either of you want to wear this hat?"

The girls exchanged a look. "I'll flip you for it," Zoe said.

Emma giggled. "Nah, go ahead. It's your grandma."

"Then you get the umbrella." Esther grabbed it from its hook beside the door. "Once we get back to the church, that is. Until then, we're going to share." She opened the door.

"But you didn't even change yet," Zoe said.

"I'm all right. I'll come back and take care of myself once we get you guys back in action." She didn't want to rush anyone, but daylight was fading. Even though no one had mentioned it lately, she knew it was on everyone's minds.

The sun would set eventually. And then what would they do?

Chapter 34
Esther

"What's wrong, Cathy?" Esther asked. Her friend was looking depressed.

Cathy sighed. "I've called every church in the state, just about. Every one with a phone number. A few of them said they would put out a call for volunteers, but it's been mostly a bust." She gestured toward the closed door. "As you can see, those called volunteers aren't exactly beating our door down."

Esther didn't know what to say, how to comfort her.

"We've had a few," Adam said. "And they're being very helpful. Though I wish those people with the dogs would show up."

"We're running out of daylight," Cathy muttered.

The front door opened, and every head in the room snapped toward it. Even Nora looked up from the Bible she'd been quietly reading in the corner.

It wasn't Levi. And it didn't look like volunteers from another church. It was four adults, two of them in police uniforms. They strode toward the desk.

"I'm Carl Pettiford, the officer in charge of this case."

Esther braced herself. She thought they were about to get in trouble. Carl wore civilian clothes. Had he been off duty when she'd called him? Carl introduced the other three people as police officers. Esther recognized the woman, who was in uniform.

"We've come to help. Give us a territory."

Adam looked dumbfounded and for several seconds didn't move. Then he came to his senses. "It seems wasteful to put you all on one team. I'd rather put each of you in charge of a team." He paused. "Would you consider that?"

Carl nodded. "Of course. Whatever you need."

Esther turned to look at Nora, who was staring at the officers with her mouth open. Esther headed her way. "Quite a development, isn't it?"

Nora looked at her with wide eyes. "You don't understand. I was praying for that exact thing the exact second they walked in. I asked God to make the police help. I mean, I know they've been helping, but I asked him to make them help *here*. With this."

"See? God is working this out. I don't know what's taking so long, but he knows, and he's got a plan."

Nora looked less skeptical than she had earlier. She got up and headed toward the map table. Her eyes met Carl's. "Thank you," she said softly.

He nodded stoically. "Just to be clear," he said in an official police-like voice. "We have no reason to think he's just hanging out somewhere on the peninsula waiting to be rescued." He let out a long breath. "But it certainly can't hurt to look."

Nora gave him a small smile.

Adam hung up his cell phone and looked at Carl. "All right. Might you be willing to go help the team currently searching the shore to the north of the Cove?" Adam sounded sheepish, as if he wasn't quite comfortable giving instructions to a police officer.

Carl looked at the area Adam was pointing to on the map and nodded. "Of course."

"Great." Adam slid a scrap of paper across the map. "Here's the number of one of the men looking."

Carl snatched it up. "Great. Thanks." And he was gone.

Adam made another phone call and assigned another officer to a team, and then

Searching

Esther looked around to see where Nora had gone off to. She was back with her Bible. Esther thought this was a great sign. If anything was going to keep this poor mother's heart intact, it was the word of God.

Esther headed toward her. "See? That's a huge addition to our team."

Nora attempted a smile, but it didn't reach her red eyes. "It's a big peninsula."

"We've already searched a fifth of it." This was a small exaggeration, but Esther didn't know the true fraction. "We'll get there." Esther heard something and turned toward the door. "What was *that*?"

"I don't know." Nora stood beside her. "It sounded like a tractor trailer truck. Do you get a lot of those on Providence Ave?"

Esther snickered. "No. Sure don't." As she headed toward the door, she heard the *whoosh* of air brakes. Whatever it was, they were stopping.

"Um, Adam?" Cathy said from the window. "Two *school buses* just pulled up."

Adam didn't respond. He looked a little dazed.

School buses? Esther's mind flitted through a half-dozen scenarios, but none of them made sense. Certainly no school had sent a busload of kids to their church.

"Oh my goodness," Cathy said slowly, still looking out the window.

Esther had never heard her sound so disbelieving.

The last police officer was on his way out and held the door open for the newcomers.

And there were a lot of them. They poured through the door, and when they stopped, Esther assumed that was the last of them, but then another surge of them burst through. They crowded into the entryway, looking around the sanctuary. It took a second for Esther to notice that they appeared to be a ragtag bunch. A lot of them wore ill-fitting, mismatched clothes. There were many ripped and stained coats. What *was* this?

A middle-aged man extricated himself from the pack, looked around as if trying to figure out who was in charge, and then headed toward Adam, extending his hand. "My name is Galen Turney." He turned to look over his shoulder, located what he was looking for, and then motioned for her to come closer. "This is my wife, Maggie." He pointed. "And those are my two boys. We're here to help. Put us to work."

Adam looked past him in wonder. "And who are the rest of you?"

Galen smiled. "This is my church."

Adam hesitated as if not sure how to proceed. Then he sprang into action. "Can you break them into teams of four or five? I'll get you some maps."

Cathy came closer to the table, her eyes as big as saucers. "What church are you from?"

It appeared that Galen didn't hear her, but another young man did. "Open Door Church from Mattawooptock."

"Oh my goodness," Cathy said quietly. "I called them hours ago."

"Well, Mattawooptock is quite a haul," Esther said.

Cathy looked at her. "Where *is* matta ... matta ... matta*what*?"

"Mattawooptock," Esther repeated. "It's over by Skowhegan."

"Wow, that's got to be a two-hour drive."

"Yes," Esther said. "Yes, it is. But they're here now. So we'd better get some more coffee on." Esther started toward the kitchenette.

"There's got to be a hundred of them," Cathy said behind her, still frozen in wonder.

Chapter 35
Nora

Nora couldn't stop weeping, and though she was still scared and exhausted, she thought these tears were mostly brought on by *hope*. Two *busloads* of people had shown up out of nowhere to help her son. She couldn't believe it. She kept looking down at her open Bible in wonder as if Jesus himself were going to spring up out of the pages and spread his arms out to hug her.

She'd been reading the Bible and praying, and four police officers had shown up. Then she'd read the Bible and prayed some more, and two *busloads* of people had shown up. She was going to keep reading the Bible and praying. Somehow she'd surfed her way back to that verse her father had highlighted. And these were more noble than those in Thessalonica, receiving the word with all readiness of mind, daily searching the scriptures if these things were so. "I have readiness of mind, now, God," she whispered. "Show me whatever you need to show me. Teach me whatever you need to teach me. I am all yours." And then she kept reading, kept praying.

Searching

And before long, she found herself back in Psalms: *Blessed be Jehovah, for he hath heard the voice of my supplications. Jehovah is my strength and my shield; my heart confided in him, and I was helped.*

Wasn't this exactly what had just happened to her? God had heard her cries. She didn't feel very strong right now, but if she had any strength at all, it wasn't coming from inside of her. And where else could it be coming from but God? What else could have guided her here to this place of help? Who else could have convinced the police officers that Levi might be nearby? Who else could have sent two busloads of volunteers from the other side of the state?

No one but God.

She didn't know much, but she knew that he was in this. And so she kept reading, and she kept praying the same prayer she'd been praying since she'd started praying: *Please save my son. Please send him help. Please bring him home.* Only now she added a new line to her prayer: *Thank you.*

Chapter 36
Esther

Esther watched this visiting pastor split up his giant group of volunteers. He seemed to be putting a great deal of thought into it, and frequently made changes to groups he'd already organized. Finally, he seemed satisfied, and he turned to face Adam. "Okay, we're ready."

"Great." Adam handed the pastor one blown up map at a time. He also handed them each a map of the whole peninsula and a list of phone numbers. "I've called back two of the teams to serve as guides for your searchers. They know the area, and they have vehicles, so they'll drive your people to where they need to be."

The pastor listened carefully, nodding.

And then they were all standing there waiting for their guides.

The church door opened so fast that it hit a few of them. Zoe and her team spilled in, and Esther thought that's the team that Adam had recalled. But they didn't act that way. With wide eyes, they looked around at all the newcomers.

"Who *are* all these people?" Emma asked.

Searching

Jason headed toward Adam and handed him the map. "Nothing."

"All right." Adam looked at each kid in turn. "Are you up for another map?"

"Wait!" Tonya strode toward them. "Can they do another map before it gets dark out?"

Adam checked his phone and then looked outside. "Probably not." He sighed. "It might not be safe out there in the dark."

"We'll be fine," Jason said tersely. "It's no more dangerous in the dark than it is in the light. And we have flashlights."

"I'll keep 'em safe, Doc," Derek said.

Esther didn't know why Derek had just called Adam "Doc" but no one else seemed to notice.

Adam chewed on his lip. "We have a lot of volunteers now. You guys can take a break if you want."

"Maybe you should," Tonya said. "You all have school tomorrow."

"We don't want a break," Jason said.

"Right," Emma chimed in.

"Then I suppose it's up to your parents." Adam looked at Tonya.

She stared at her daughter. "I suppose I have to trust God to protect you." Then she looked at Jason. "And I'm trusting *you* too. You keep her right beside you."

"We will," Zoe and Jason said in unison.

Derek had returned to the doughnut boxes.

"All right. Call us if you need anything or if it gets too dark." Adam nodded toward the door just as the Puddy team came back in.

Roderick looked at the crowd. "Wow. Welcome, everyone! Thanks for coming."

A murmur traveled through the cluster.

Adam came out from behind his map table to assign each Puddy parent to one of the teams, and two teams left with new maps.

The new pastor looked at Adam. "There are more guides coming?'

"Absolutely. They should be here any second."

The pastor nodded. "Excellent." He looked at his watch.

"Who ate all the doughnuts?" Derek cried, as if he was being personally persecuted.

There had been a *lot* of doughnuts, and Esther didn't see how they could all be gone already. She thought Derek must have been mistaken and headed that way to find the man a doughnut but then she noticed that a lot of the Mattawooptock folks appeared to be chewing.

"Go join your team, Derek. I'll go get you some more doughnuts." It took her a minute to locate her purse, but then she was on her way out the door.

When she walked through the door of the coffee shop, the young man behind the counter looked frightened. "We've only just taken the newest batch out of the fryer."

Esther nodded. "That's all right. Give me what you've got please." She plunked her purse down on the counter and reached in for her wallet.

"But they're not going to be frosted or glazed, because they're too hot." He was nearing full panic mode.

"That's all right. I'll take them plain or however you can give them."

Beyond bewildered, he turned away to go fill her order.

She looked into her wallet and was dismayed to see that this delivery was going to wipe her out. Oh well. She would worry about tomorrow tomorrow.

Chapter 37
Zoe

"Again, I think we should go see Kendall," Zoe said.

Jason didn't answer her, and she looked to see if he had heard her. He was grinding his jaw. Finally, he said, "I'm sorry. I just don't think he'd tell us anything."

"I could try to beat it out of him," Derek offered with a lackadaisical air as if he'd just suggested he could offer him tea.

Jason's face registered a small panic. "I don't think that's the way Jesus wants us to do it."

Zoe looked back at Derek in time to see him shrug. Then he looked out the window and started singing "Santa Claus Is Coming to Town."

She didn't want to beat Kendall up, but still she thought it was a good idea to go talk to him at least. And even if it wasn't a good idea, what could it hurt? It would cost them time, sure, but not much. Trouble was, she didn't know how to convince Jason. So she stopped trying. "What's our next area?"

Searching

He showed her the map. "Pretty close to town this time. We'll probably have to knock on some doors."

Zoe looked at her phone. The battery was at seventeen percent. "I'd better plug in my phone then." She would need to use it to show people Levi's photo.

"Yeah, we all should make sure our phones are charged up because we're going to need them for flashlights," Jason said.

Derek stopped singing to say, "My phone battery never dies." Then he started singing again.

They parked at an intersection on the edge of town and climbed back out into the rain. Zoe was running on fumes. Whether or not this searching took them all night, she still fully intended to skip school tomorrow. She realized that they might still not have found Levi by morning, and this thought scared her so much that she pushed it out of her mind. If he hadn't been found by morning, she wouldn't be sleeping in. She'd still be searching. She looked at her friends. She was pretty sure the same was true of them.

"I'll take the backyards," Derek said. "People don't want to see me coming to their front doors."

Zoe wasn't sure if this would truly alarm anyone. He wasn't that scary looking. But she'd also grown used to him.

"It's probably not a good idea to get caught sneaking around in their backyards either," Jason said, but Derek was already out of sight. Jason shook his head. "That guy."

"If we're just knocking on doors," Zoe said, "we should split up. It'll be faster." In no way did she want to go knock on strangers' doors alone, but she was in a hurry. She was positive he wasn't in this area, and thought it was a waste of time. They needed to get back to searching where there were no people.

"Okay." Jason sounded reluctant. "But stay in sight of each other."

They started walking, but Emma didn't move.

Jason stopped and looked back at her.

"Sorry, I really don't want to be knocking on doors alone."

"No prob," Zoe said quickly. "Come with me, Emma. We'll use your phone for his picture."

Emma looked relieved.

"You take that side of the street." Jason pointed with his chin. "I'll stay over here."

Great. Give me the side that has Derek sneaking around in backyards.

Searching

No one answered at the first house, though the girls allowed plenty of time. As they walked down the steps, they made eye contact with Jason. It appeared he'd had the same experience.

At the next house, it was obvious people were home. The driveway was full of cars, and she could hear a television. Yet no one would come to the door.

Awesome. This was going to be super helpful.

Someone did answer at the third house, and she politely looked at the photograph on Emma's phone. Then she shook her head. Sorry, she hadn't seen him.

At the fourth house, a woman called her whole family to the door to look at the picture, but no one recognized him. Then she asked if they needed any help looking.

Zoe blinked, surprised. "Yes, that would be great. We're organizing out of New Beginnings Church. If you go there, they'll assign you an official area to search."

The woman turned her head and hollered. "Get your boots and raincoats on, everyone!" Then she looked back to Zoe. "New Beginnings Church? Never heard of it."

"It's the old, abandoned church on Providence Ave."

"Oh yeah? I thought that place was condemned."

Zoe shook her head. "Not even close."

Chapter 38
Zoe

"You know," Zoe said to Jason. They'd just climbed back into the car.

Jason started the engine and cranked the heat. It was now full on dark, it was still raining, and it was very cold. "Yes, I know. We are pretty close to Kendall's house."

"Yes, we are."

"Let's do it. Seriously, Jason," Derek said. "We've got to find this kid. It's going to be cold out tonight."

Jason nodded. "All right, but if things get weird, we bail."

Zoe didn't understand what the big deal was. Kendall was a creep, but he wasn't anything to fear. At least, she didn't think so.

Jason shut his lights off before he even pulled into the driveway.

"Are you trying to sneak up on him?" Zoe asked, trying to lighten the mood.

"No, I'm trying not to annoy his psycho father."

Oh. Maybe *that* was something to fear. Zoe didn't know Kendall had a psycho father. She climbed out of the warm car and followed Jason toward the house. Derek stepped up beside Jason, and Zoe looked back at Emma, who was carefully watching her feet as she tried to navigate the puddles. Zoe reached back and touched her arm, tucking the younger girl behind her. "Stay close," she said.

A man, probably Kendall's father, swung the door open before Jason had even knocked. He looked Jason up and down and then belted over his shoulder. "Kendall, friends are here."

Zoe didn't see Jason flinch, but she still knew he had.

The man wasn't wearing a shirt, and Zoe didn't understand how anybody could have that much hair on his chest. He took a drink from the beer can in his hand and then turned and walked away, leaving the door open. He hadn't invited them to step inside, and none of them made a move to. Zoe thought they'd probably all rather stand outside in the rain.

They waited and waited, but Kendall never came. Eventually, someone inside shut the door. Zoe didn't know if they'd forgotten they were outside or if they had meant to slam the door in their faces.

"I told you," Jason said. "Waste of time." He turned to walk away and nearly ran into Zoe.

Searching

But Derek stepped up to the door and pounded on it. Then, he hollered at them to open the door, using several colorful expletives to help convey the urgency of his request.

Jason looked horrified. Zoe was thrilled. Emma giggled. The door opened.

It was Kendall, looking worse for wear. Either he was drunk, or something was very very wrong. "What?"

"Where's Levi?" Derek asked.

Kendall took a step back and wiped his mouth with the back of his hand. "Levi who?"

Derek stepped onto the threshold, and his posture was menacing. Zoe started to fear he really might hit the kid, and though she didn't care one iota about Kendall, she wasn't sure how that would turn out should Kendall's father, or other people who might be nearby, get involved.

"Tell me where he is!" Derek thundered.

Zoe backed up, bumping into Emma. She didn't have the wherewithal to apologize, though.

The shirtless man reappeared behind Kendall and swore. "What is this?" he shouted.

"We need to get out of here," Zoe muttered to Jason.

"I know." Jason sounded young and scared. He reached out to grab Derek's sleeve, but Derek yanked his arm away from Jason's touch.

Apparently, the shirtless man interpreted this motion as a coming blow, because he grabbed Kendall's shoulder and threw him behind him like a ragdoll.

Derek widened his stance, and the shirtless man swung his fist.

Zoe looked away, bracing herself as if she were the one about to be hit. She heard skin on skin, but then nothing else. She forced herself to look and saw Derek standing right where he had been. He'd been punched, she was sure of it, but it hadn't done much damage.

The shirtless man also appeared confused. Why hadn't Derek hit him back?

"Dad, stop," Kendall said weakly, finding his feet. "Just shut the door."

"I'm not leaving till you tell me where Levi is, you little punk."

Kendall's dad looked back at his son. "Do you know where Levi is?"

"No."

Kendall's dad looked at Derek. "Is he missing or something?"

Derek nodded. "Since Wednesday."

What? Had Derek just exaggerated for effect or did he really not know the days of the week? Zoe figured either was possible.

"No, *Friday*, you moron," Kendall said.

Zoe's breath caught. Had Derek just set that little trap on purpose? No way.

"And where was he on Friday?' Derek asked levelly.

Not appearing to realize his mistake, Kendall again claimed to not know anything.

Derek turned his attention to the father. "Levi's mom is worried sick. Your boy knows where that boy is. Why don't we shut this door and give you a minute to let him tell you." Derek's words were loaded with extra meaning, but Zoe didn't know if that extra meaning was getting through to Kendall's dad.

"No need." The dad turned to his son. "Tell me where he is right now. Or else."

"I don't know," Kendall said slowly and convincingly. Then he called Levi a few choice words.

Zoe didn't know Levi well, but she was pretty sure he didn't deserve any of them. Before she knew what was happening, Kendall's dad had backhanded him across the face. Then he straddled him, grabbed him by the front of his shirt and shook him.

Kendall let out a tirade of gibberish. He was obviously drunk. He was obviously scared. What he said made no sense.

"Derek," Zoe said, but then didn't know what else to say. She wanted to tell him to stop the man from hurting Kendall, but she didn't know what words to use.

But then it was over as quickly as it started. The man let go of Kendall's shirt, and Kendall flopped back onto the floor. His father straightened up, turned toward Derek, and grabbed the door. "He doesn't know anything." He swore again. "Get out of my house."

Derek backed up a step. "Sorry to bother you." He turned and stepped out of the house, and the door slammed behind him. Derek started toward the car, singing "Jingle Bells."

Zoe looked at Jason with wide eyes.

"Yeah. Coming here was a great idea." Jason started after Derek.

Zoe's stomach churned. Great. It wasn't bad enough looking for a kid who might be dead. It wasn't bad enough being cold and scared and tired and hungry. Now Jason was mad at her too. She forced her feet to start walking and told herself that she could cry about that later. Again, Levi didn't have time for her angst.

Searching

As soon as she shut the car door behind her, though, Jason apologized. "I'm not mad at you. I'm mad at everyone else. And I'm embarrassed."

"What?" Zoe really wanted to understand.

Jason lowered his voice. "I can't believe I couldn't get my teammates to help. I haven't been able to get anyone to help. And I haven't been able to help myself. And now Derek has accomplished more than I have." He sighed.

She wanted to comfort him but didn't know how. So she busied herself checking her phone. "Uh, Jason? I don't think your charger works. My phone is at one percent now."

Jason groaned. "There's no good service here, either, so that probably drained it even faster."

"Oh no," Emma said. "Mine's almost dead too."

"Jason, we need to get out of here," Derek said.

"You're right." Jason started the car. "Wait."

"Nahhh," Derek said. "I don't think we should wait here."

Jason put the car in reverse and started backing up.

"What is it?" Zoe asked. She knew he'd thought of something.

"Probably nothing."

"What's probably nothing?"
"I think I know where Levi is."

Chapter 39
Esther

The doors opened, and three teams flooded in. Most of the people went straight to the doughnuts. A few went to report in at the map table. Esther drifted that way to hear the news.

There wasn't any. Everyone was soaked, it was dark, and they hadn't seen anything. They readily took the next map, though, and after refilling coffee cups and using the bathrooms, back outside they went.

One of the police-led teams came in and followed a similar routine. They were on their way out the door when Carl Pettiford came in with his team. He spent a long time looking at the map. "We're actually making progress," he said, and Esther wasn't sure who he was talking to. Maybe himself. "That's if people aren't missing clues. And that's if he's holding still." He looked up and rubbed the back of his neck. "I hope people aren't damaging evidence."

Evidence that no one ever would have found, Esther thought but didn't vocalize.

"It's rained pretty hard since Friday," Carl said, still mostly to himself. "These people probably won't damage anything that the rain wouldn't have washed away anyway."

Adam, wisely, Esther thought, made no attempt to participate in this one-sided conversation. He stood there quietly.

"All right." Carl held his hand out. "Give me the next map."

Adam handed him one.

"What about that area?" Carl pointed at the map, at a shoreline area surrounded by pencil shadings. Everything nearby had already been searched.

"I've been informed that this area is mostly rocks and cliffs. I didn't think we should be out there in the dark."

Carl put his new map down. "Give me that one. I can do it." He nodded eagerly. "I'll keep my team safe. And then we'll have that entire section searched. We'll know he's not on that side of the peninsula."

Adam looked hesitant, but he traded the maps out. "Okay. Godspeed."

Something like amusement flickered across Carl's face, but then he hollered to his team and headed for the door.

Esther looked at Adam. "Do you need anything?"

He said no, but he looked tired.

Searching

"All right. I'm heading back to the prayer circle. But you holler if you need me." She turned and walked toward the corner of the sanctuary.

Nora fell into step beside her. "Can I join you?" She clutched the big study Bible tightly to her chest.

"Of course."

They slipped into two folding metal chairs. Vera looked up at them and gave Esther a small smile. Esther didn't think Vera had moved from her chair since they'd formed the circle. Esther scanned the circle. Come to think of it, she didn't think Vicky or Rachel had moved either. Wow, they must be exhausted. Esther bowed her head to join them.

Only minutes later, Esther heard the commotion of other teams spilling into the sanctuary. She resisted the urge to go see what they were reporting. If they'd found anything, she would hear about it. For now, she was right where she needed to be.

There was a lull in the praying, and Esther took a deep breath. "Father in heaven, we thank you for the many blessings you've given in the last few hours. Thank you for the Mattawooptock folks. Thank you for the local volunteers. Thank you for sending the police officers. And thank you for a mother's love.

Thank you for Nora's heart. Thank you for what you've given her through your word to sustain her in these difficult minutes. Thank you for her faith, for her love, for her perseverance. Please give her a peace that passes understanding as she waits to hold her son in her arms. In Jesus' precious name we pray."

Nora slid her hand into Esther's and squeezed.

Esther squeezed back.

Chapter 40
Zoe

"What do you mean you know where he is?" Zoe cried.

"Well, I don't know for sure," Jason backpedaled. "It was just something that Kendall said at the end there."

"What Kendall said at the end made no sense," Zoe said. Was Jason cracking under all this pressure? "He was scared of his father and started drunk babbling." She should know. She'd drunk babbled a time or two herself.

"You're probably right, but do you guys mind if I check something out? It's close-by."

Zoe hesitated. What was he up to? "If you have a lead, we should probably tell the people at church."

"It's not a lead. Like you said, Kendall wasn't making any sense. I don't want to get everyone excited. If I'm wrong, then no harm done. If I'm right, though, I'd rather know sooner than later."

"All right. What did he say?"

Jason looked at her, but she couldn't read his expression in the dark. "Did anyone else hear him use the phrase 'devil's house'?"

"Yeah," Derek said. "He said they'd shoved the devil's house together."

"Who's they?" Zoe asked.

"And how do you shove a house?" Emma added.

"I think he might have meant to say they *left* together," Derek said. "But I didn't know that devil's house meant something. Does it, Jason?"

"I'm not sure." Jason turned onto a dirt road. "But there's an old house that some people claim to have partied in. I've heard it called that. I've heard it called devil's house."

"And do you know where it is?" Zoe asked.

"Sort of. I don't even know if it's real. That's why I don't want to go out on a limb, here, but I've been told where it is." He took his foot off the accelerator. "If I can remember."

"And are we going there with only one flashlight?" Emma asked nervously.

"Shoot," Jason said. "Maybe we should go back to the church first."

"What's your battery at?" Zoe asked.

"I don't know. Check."

Feeling a small thrill at touching Jason's phone, she checked. "You're almost full." Must be nice to have a new phone. She resisted the urge to shoot Alita a quick I-think-we-should-break-up text. She put the phone down before she did just that. "We're almost there, right? Wherever *there* is. Let's go see if the house is even real. If we find something, we'll call in the calvary."

Derek snickered. "You mean cavalry?"

Zoe was embarrassed. "Whatever."

"Yeah," Derek said, sounding contemplative. "Might be smarter to call in Calvary."

Jason pulled his car onto a very narrow road.

"Is this even a road?" Emma asked.

"Used to be, I think," Jason said, not sounding sure of himself.

Road or not, it was incredibly rough, and they bounced around as Jason made the sloping climb. When he hit a bump that made a sickening scraping sound on the bottom of his car, he stopped. "Maybe we go the rest of the way on foot."

"The rest of the way to what?" Zoe was looking through the windshield and didn't see anything promising. Of course, she couldn't see anything at all. There could well be something promising out there in the wet darkness.

"There's supposed to be a house up here. Or there used to be. Now it's abandoned, supposedly."

"And they named it the devil's house?" Derek asked. "Just for kicks?"

Jason turned the car off, but he left the headlights on. "Supposedly people have done satanic stuff up there." He seemed to suddenly remember Emma. "Not real satanic stuff, though. They were just stupid kids. Trying to pretend to be brave."

Jason climbed out of the car then, and Zoe wished *she* were a little better at pretending to be brave. She looked back at Emma. "I'll wait here by the car with you if you want."

Emma shook her head rapidly and leapt out of the car.

So much for that ploy. Zoe climbed back out and once again stood in the rain. Jason started walking, and she followed, her wet socks making each step a squishy affair. When this was over, she was going to go hang out in a desert. She'd heard there was a desert of Maine. She'd never been there, but right now it sounded like the best possible place to be. Maybe she could winter there, hibernating like a bear. Only in the desert.

Soon, the headlights didn't seem so powerful. "Are you sure your battery won't die?" she asked, a little out of breath from the uphill climb.

"No," Jason said shortly. He was moving faster now. Was he in a hurry to get where they were going so he could then return to his car, or did he sense they were close to something? "I'm not sure of anything."

Derek started singing, "We Three Kings."

Zoe found it oddly comforting.

Chapter 41
Levi

Had he just heard a car? Levi held his breath to listen. No, it was just the rain. Still, he was reluctant to breathe again, afraid he'd miss something. *You've got to breathe*, he reminded himself, *or you'll die.* He took long, controlled breaths, trying to be quiet, trying to listen. But the car sound didn't come again. Maybe he'd imagined it. It's not like he was close to a road or anything.

Maybe he should try to get some sleep. Then morning would come faster, if he lived that long. For the millionth time, he wished his Gamp was still there. His loneliness was now the most painful part of his situation.

Please, God. Please send help. If I'm going to die here, please help me to accept that and do it bravely. And if I die here, please help them to find me quickly, so that my mother doesn't have to wonder what happened to me. But I don't really want to die here, so if possible, could you get someone here before I do?

Chapter 42
Zoe

They could still see the headlights behind them, but those headlights were no longer helping them to see what was in front of them. Jason took his phone out and turned on the flashlight, but the light of one phone alone—no matter how fancy the phone—was pathetically weak because of the rain.

"We need to bring the car up here," Derek said matter-of-factly.

Jason turned to look down the hill. "I don't think it will make it up here."

"It will." Derek started that way. "I'll go get it."

"Do you have a driver's license?"

Derek laughed shrilly and started singing "Chestnuts Roasting on an Open Fire."

Jason appeared to be frozen with indecision.

Zoe stepped closer to him. She wanted to take his hand, and though she thought she could probably get away with it under the circumstances, she didn't quite dare. "He'll be fine. How much damage can he do driving up a narrow road?" She could've added, *And how much is that junk car worth, anyway?* but she didn't.

He gave her side-eye. "He could rip the bottom off my car. The guy's nuts." He exhaled shakily. "And then I'll have you two girls stranded out here in creepville."

Part of her was annoyed at his blatant sexism. Part of her was thrilled that he felt protective of her. Her *and Emma*, sure, but still, it was worth something.

The car started, and the headlights started moving toward them—quickly. She felt Jason stiffen beside her.

"Holy cow," Emma muttered.

The old car flew up the hill, and the headlights bounced around like ping-pong balls. "Stop!" Jason screamed, throwing his hands up into the air. It was doubtful Derek could've heard the shout, but he might see the arms.

He didn't slow down. If anything, he sped up.

"Stop!" Jason shouted again. Then he let his arms fall and muttered, "I'm going to kill him."

"Wait till *after* we find Levi," Emma said through chattering teeth.

Zoe looked at her. "Are you okay?"

"I'm fine," Emma said quickly.

Searching

The car stopped in front of them, and Derek stuck his head out of the window. "Get out of the road. I'll keep going, and you guys follow." He rolled up the window and started driving before they had even moved. He had turned the radio on. It was playing Christmas music. What radio station was already playing Christmas music? Or did Derek know of some station that specialized in annoying her?

They struggled to keep up.

"Maybe we should get back in the car?" Zoe said. It felt like she wore buckets of water for shoes, which made even a slight uphill climb a lot more work.

"No, it would weigh the car down, make the bumps worse," Jason said.

Zoe bristled. Had he just called her heavy? She slapped the thought out of her mind.

They walked and walked. "How long is this stupid road?" Zoe asked.

"I have no idea," Jason said. "But I don't think we've gone very far, even if it feels like it."

Awesome.

After what felt like another thousand steps, and at least a dozen horrible scraping sounds coming from Jason's car—one time she could have sworn she saw sparks—Zoe started to seriously think about giving up. They still had to get back *out* of these woods. With their one old car with limited gas and their one flashlight.

She opened her mouth to announce this idea, but something stopped her. She didn't want Jason to think she was a wuss. She didn't want Emma, a thirteen-year-old, to be tougher than her. She realized that she even cared what *Derek* thought, which was ridiculous. Why did she care what he thought? So she didn't announce her idea, and this made her angry with herself. The anger made her more tired. Each step made her more resentful. What had she gotten herself into? Yet another awful experience in the name of following Jason around.

"Look!" Emma cried.

Zoe had been watching her feet so studiously that when she looked up, her neck expressed gratitude. Sure enough, lit by their headlights: a very old house. A shiver traveled down her spine. She realized the car had stopped.

Jason stepped closer to Derek's window. "Get a little closer, would you?"

Derek nodded, an uncharacteristically serious look on his face. He wasn't singing now. He crept closer to the house, and the others followed on foot. Zoe realized she was holding her breath and forced herself to breathe.

"Levi?" Emma called.

Zoe jumped.

"Levi!" Emma said even louder, not giving him enough time to respond between calls. Emma held a hand up. "Did you hear that? Turn off the car!" she screamed at Derek, who immediately obeyed.

The three of them stood stock-still. All Zoe could hear was water falling on wet leaves. She'd never realized how deafening that sound was.

"There!" Emma called. "Levi! We hear you! Hang on!"

"Emma," Jason said levelly. "I don't hear anything."

"Well, you're deaf," Emma said, and took off running toward the terrifying house in front of them.

Chapter 43
Levi

The first time Levi heard his name, he was certain he was imagining things again. That wasn't Gamp's voice, though. It was a girl's voice. He didn't recognize it.

But then it came again. He tried to cry out in response, but "I'm here" sounded more like a grunt than actual words.

He stretched up to try to look out the window, and though he couldn't see anything but treetops, he was almost certain those treetops were lit up by something. He called out again. "Here! Help!" This time, his cry more resembled actual words.

Suddenly everything got quieter. There had been an engine running. He hadn't noticed that noise with all the rain, but he noticed the absence of it. *Thank you, God.* There was a vehicle here. There was a girl's voice. *Thank you, God.* And they'd turned off the engine, so they didn't plan on driving away. At least, not yet. He couldn't let them leave. He screamed, "Help!" as loud as he could. His head swam with pain, which was followed by nausea. He slid back down to the floor, trying not to retch. He knew he didn't have anything in his stomach to throw up, but dry heaving hurt worse than just about anything.

"I hear you, Levi!" the girl said.

He tried to respond, but he couldn't.

He couldn't do anything. *Please*, he silently cried to God. *Please*.

Chapter 44
Zoe

"Emma, wait!" Jason took off after her, and Derek leapt out of the car to do the same.

Feeling left out, Zoe hurried toward the building. Again, she gave in to watching her feet, so sure that she would slip and fall if she didn't, so she didn't see much of interest until she realized the others had stopped and she applied the brakes. She looked up. The front door stood open.

Jason gently moved Emma aside so he could go first. He shined his light into the house. Emma grabbed his sleeve and went with him. Derek went next and when he got a glimpse inside, he swore.

"Smells like garbage in here," Jason muttered.

"Levi!" Emma cried. "Are you down there?"

Jason gave it a few seconds and then whispered, "Did you hear him?"

Zoe didn't understand what was happening and tried to get a better look. The trouble was, they were not going into the house, and they were clogging the doorway. She was a tall girl, but she wasn't quite tall enough to see

Searching

over Derek's winter cap. "What is it?" she whispered.

Surprisingly, Derek stepped aside so she could see. Her breath caught. *Oh no.* The wooden floor had completely caved in. Boards sloped down at various angles, creating a jarringly discordant image. Had Levi fallen through *that*? If so, he might have been stabbed by any number of those broken boards. "Did you hear anything?" she asked Emma, who apparently had superhuman hearing.

Emma shook her head. "Levi?" she called again softly. Then, "I think I heard him."

"You think?" Jason said. He looked down at her. "You're the only one who has heard anything. Are you sure? Maybe he's not even here."

"He's here," Emma snapped, and Zoe unequivocally believed her. She didn't know Emma *that* well, but she knew her well enough.

Jason turned back to the broken floor. He shined his light toward the ceiling, which had a gaping hole in it. "Well no wonder. For how many years has the rain and snow been hitting this floor directly?"

Zoe saw that the walls had been spray painted with weird symbols. Were those supposed to be satanic? They looked like little kids had gotten a hold of some paint cans. Apparently, only red and black ones. "I believe you, Emma."

Jason sighed. "I do too. I guess. He's got to be in the basement, but how on earth are we going to get to him?"

"We said we'd call when we found him," Zoe said quickly. "We found him, so call. The fire department can get him out easy."

"Good idea!" Jason looked down at his phone and groaned. "I have no signal."

"Try it anyway," Zoe said.

"It's not that I have no bars," Jason said, sounding annoyed. "I actually have the no signal symbol." He held his phone over his shoulder so she could see it.

She still thought he should try, but she didn't say that.

He tried. She saw him punch in 9-1-1. And she saw that he was right. No service.

"That's all right," Derek said. "I think we can get him out."

"How?" Jason sounded incredulous.

"I have no idea."

"Give me your phone." Before he could stop her, Emma snatched Jason's phone out of his hand and ran away, leaving them with only the dim light of the car's headlights, which did nothing to show the floor they somehow had to navigate.

"Emma!" Jason scolded and turned to follow her.

Zoe and Derek exchanged a look and then did the same.

They found Emma not far from the door, on her hands and knees, shining the flashlight through one of the basement windows.

"Do you see anything?" Jason asked.

"No."

Poor Emma. She sounded so disappointed.

"Levi!" she called through the window. Then she turned her head to get her ears closer to the filthy glass. "I hear him!" she cried. "We hear you, Levi! Hang on! We'll come get you out." She scrambled to her feet and ran around the house.

"Where is she going?" Jason mumbled and followed, running one hand along the wall of the building.

They rounded the corner to find her again on her hands and knees. "I see him," she said, sounding as if she didn't quite believe it herself. This window wasn't a window anymore. It was just a hole, and she had stuck her head inside. "Levi?" she said. "He's not moving." She pulled her head out and looked up at Jason. "What do we do?"

Jason took his phone away from Emma and looked at the screen as if he hoped some bars had appeared since they'd walked around the house. Apparently, none had because he didn't try to call anyone. He let the phone drop to his side and looked at Derek. "Do you have any ideas?"

For a second Zoe was offended that he hadn't asked her but then she realized she had exactly zero ideas and was grateful he'd picked Derek.

Derek chewed on his lip for a minute. "I think you should go get help."

"And leave you here?" Jason said warily.

"Do we have any rope?" Emma asked.

"What are we going to do with rope?" Jason's patronizing tone annoyed Zoe on Emma's behalf, but she didn't seem to notice it.

"I could go in through the window and tie it around him."

Jason pointed his light at the window. "I don't think you can fit through there."

"If he's injured," Derek said, "we shouldn't be dragging him or pulling him. He probably fell through the floor, right? So he could have a neck injury or a back injury. If he's not moving, those are both real possibilities."

Emma's face jerked toward the window.

"What is it?" Jason asked.

"I heard him moan." She stuck her head back into the basement. "Levi?" She made a weird blowing noise. "Gross! There are so many cobwebs!"

Zoe shuddered.

She looked back to Jason. "He's not answering me. I'm going to go in and check on him."

"What? No! Then we'll have two of you trapped in a basement."

"*I* won't be trapped, you goofball," Emma said. "I'm not injured. I can just crawl back out."

"No!" Jason appeared flustered. "I forbid it!"

Emma let out the cutest little rebellious giggle, one that made Zoe immensely proud of her. "Nice try. I'm going in." She stuck her head through the hole, and started to wiggle in.

"Wait!" Zoe cried. Was the girl crazy?

"What? Are you going to try to stop me too?"

"No! Pull your head out!"

Emma obliged, but she looked impatient. "What?"

"You should go in feet first. Here I'll hold your hands." She knelt in front of the window.

Chapter 45
Zoe

"Zoe! Don't encourage this!" Jason said, but Zoe tried to ignore him.

She didn't know if this was the right move, but since she didn't know what the right move *was,* she thought it was more important to actually *move* than to hem and haw about moving. They had to do *something.* Levi could be dying in there for all they knew.

Understanding dawned, and Emma nodded eagerly. She swung her body around with catlike agility and then grabbed one of Zoe's hands in a death grip. Emma's hand was cold and wet. Zoe squeezed it tightly, trying to convey that she had her.

Emma stuck one foot back through the hole. "Man, this is awkward." She pushed on the ground with her free hand and stuck her other foot in through the hole, her thighs resting on the rotten sill, which collapsed a bit under her weight. Zoe edged closer as Emma started to disappear in through the hole. Zoe started to have trepidations—a fine time to start with that—and said, "Don't worry, I can get you out. No matter what."

Emma didn't look at her. She was too busy looking under her arm at the hole. "I'm not worried."

How had this kid gotten so brave? She was acting more and more like Mary Sue.

She'd squiggled in far enough so that her belly was the fulcrum. She grunted softly. "Okay, here we go. Please try not to let go of me." She pushed up hard with her left hand, lifting her belly off the windowsill and squiggled backward like an ambitious worm. Zoe scooted forward to keep up, and gravity took over. Emma let out a little cry of pain.

"You okay?"

"Yeah," she said, not sounding okay at all. "I haven't hit the floor yet."

Oh no. She was just dangling there by her arm? With her free hand, Zoe grabbed Emma's forearm as she scooted all the way to the wall.

"You're squeezing too tight!" Emma squeaked, and Zoe relaxed her grip, but only a little.

Emma's weight pulled Zoe's arms into the building; her neck was pressed against the slimy, cold wall. She tilted her head to prevent her cheek from touching the house, and then the weight was gone.

"I found the floor!" Emma cried, and then she ripped her hand out of Zoe's clutch, and Zoe heard her footsteps.

Zoe plopped her hands onto the wet ground and stuck her head in.

"What do you see?" Jason asked.

She saw Levi, and he didn't look good. He was mostly lying down, with his head upright against the wall as if he'd once been sitting but had slithered down.

"Levi?" Emma tentatively touched his shoulder. "Levi? Can you hear me?" She paused and then cried out, "He's breathing, but his lips are blue!" She grabbed his hand. "Oh my goodness, he is so cold!" She ripped off Gramma's jacket and threw it over him. Then she looked up at Zoe with wide eyes. "We need to get him out of here! Quick!" Emma looked up at the hole over her head and gasped. "A giant wood stove came crashing down through the floor." Zoe could almost hear Emma's wheels turning. "If I can get him up on that, you guys might be able to pull him up through the hole."

Zoe found this plan one hundred percent impossible. How was little Emma going to get a nearly unconscious teenage boy up onto a stove? She tried to think of a gentle way to tell her that.

Jason took over, and he didn't try to be gentle. "That's insane, Emma," he hollered. "Can he move on his own?"

She didn't answer, which was answer enough.

"You're not going to be able to move him," Jason hollered and then said more quietly to Zoe, "Are there stairs?"

Zoe looked around. "There used to be."

"What does that mean? Are they usable?"

Zoe tried to imagine how they could be. "I don't think so. And the floor at the top of the stairs is gone. Emma might be able to climb up them, and that's a big might, but I don't see how she's going to get Levi up them."

"Don't worry, Levi," Emma said softly, and Zoe thought she could hear tears in her voice. "We're going to get you out of here. We just need to figure out a plan."

"I could do it," Zoe said before she could think about it.

"No *way* are you fitting through that window," Jason said.

If he called her fat one more time this evening, she was going to shove *him* into a rotten basement. And leave him there.

"I wasn't going to try to go through the window," she said, formulating the plan as she spoke. "I'll go in through the top."

"What? That's insane! That's how Levi got into this mess!"

"She said the wood stove fell through. So, we find the chimney. Then we know where the wood stove is. Then I go in, hugging the wall, straight for the chimney. Then I lower myself down. I don't fall. I am controlled the whole time." She tried to sound confident, but she wasn't. Zoe had fallen through a lot of windows in her day. And with her long limbs, she wasn't graceful or coordinated. She didn't know if she could make this work, but she didn't see any other option, and they needed to do *something.*

"No," Jason said firmly. "This is stupid. We go get help."

"I don't know if he has time for that," Emma said. "He doesn't look so good. We need to get him warmed up."

"Esther is going to kill me," Jason said. "Literally kill me."

"It could work," Derek said, and Jason groaned. "We need to see the area around where the stove was first. Because if we can't pull him out and get him out of the house, there's no point in getting him onto the wood stove."

That was an excellent point.

"Hang on, Emma," Derek hollered. "We're going to the kitchen."

They left without waiting for Zoe, so she scrambled to her feet and followed. She got to the front door just in time to hear Derek say, "It's possible." She peeked into the room. She had no idea how Derek knew this had ever been a kitchen. There were no appliances left, and she didn't see any sink. Remnants of a counter hung off one wall; maybe that's what he was basing his theory on.

"We passed the chimney on the way here," Zoe said. "So the stove should be on that wall." She pointed, and they both looked. A stovepipe chimney hung suspended from the wall, with no stove attached. Under the chimney, the floor had been ripped completely from the wall.

"There's nowhere for you to stand," Jason said.

"Yes, there is." Zoe was feeling stubborn now. Whether this was a good plan or not, she wanted to see it through. "I don't have to get directly over the stove. Just close enough to jump on it."

Jason looked at her with wide eyes. "You're going to jump onto a stove?"

He had a point. This did sound a mite unrealistic. "Yes, I'm going to jump onto the stove."

Something that might have been admiration glittered in his eyes.

"I admire your hutzpah," Derek said, "but maybe I should do that part."

Something like relief swept through her.

"No offense, Derek," Jason said, "but who has more strength to pull the kid out—you or Zoe?"

Derek swore. Then he started humming "All I Want for Christmas Is My Two Front Teeth."

"That's not helping," Jason muttered.

Derek stopped humming to say, "It's helping me." He continued humming.

"Come on. Let's do this." Zoe wanted to get to Levi before he died, but she also wanted to get this over with before she lost her courage. She pushed past the men and stepped onto the threshold. A chill raced over her. Devil's house or no, this place *was* creepy. She couldn't believe Levi had chosen to hang out here on purpose. Then images of creepy places she'd frequented flashed through her mind. Oh yeah. Until recently, she too had occasionally wanted to find a hiding place.

She stepped inside and to the left, pressing her butt into the wall. She wasn't truly scared until she removed her right foot from the threshold. Then she was standing on the smallest, most tenuous lip, staring at a downward slide into a dark hole. "Emma?"

"We're here."

"We're coming!"

"We know. We can hear every word!"

Despite it all, Zoe laughed at this, and the laughter lifted most of her fear away. *Just focus*, she told herself and sidestepped toward the stove wall. She put most of her weight on her left foot and waited to see if the floor would give way. She looked nervously at the hole. It wasn't the fall that scared her. It was encountering all those jagged edges on the way down. Maybe they should have smashed the floor to smithereens before attempting this quest. Oh well, too late now. She pulled her right foot in alongside her left and exhaled. Good. She was still on the first floor. She pressed her fingers into the wall behind her, as if this would help anything.

"You're doing great," Derek whispered.

Was he afraid that the vibrations of his voice might make the floor collapse? She looked down. He might not be wrong. She slid her left foot to the left, taking a bigger stride this time, pushed on the floor, and then, when it didn't make a cracking sound, brought her right foot alongside.

"I can see you!" Emma cried. "I can see your feet!"

Zoe took another step, feeling more confident now. And then another. She had reached the corner of the room. She peered through the hole, trying to see the wood stove. She wished Emma had a flashlight to shine on it, but alas, their search party had left search-and-rescue headquarters without a real flashlight among them. When this was over, she was going to *beg* her grandmother for a new phone. She would need one while she was in the hospital, recuperating from two broken legs. She turned her body and stuck her left leg out. She pushed on the lip of floor that was left along the chimney wall. This section of the wall felt squishier. It had a little give to it, but only a little, less than an inch. She hesitated, not sure what to do. Did she want to turn back now after she'd come this far? No, definitely not. But did she want to turn back before she *couldn't* turn back? Maybe. She looked at Jason, who looked impossibly far away.

She could read his face like a book. He was impressed. She looked at her feet. Very well, then. She would continue. Only partially aware that she was once again making decisions based on Jason's actions and facial expressions, she took another step. The floor sagged beneath her weight, but it did not give way. Before she could talk herself out of it, she took another step.

And then she saw it. At least, she thought she did. Why hadn't she taken Jason's flashlight? "Shine your light over here," she whispered.

He did, but it didn't help much. She was still looking into a black hole, and it looked as though part of that blackness was raised above the rest. She thought that was the wood stove. "I'm almost there," she whispered.

"But you're not to the chimney yet," Jason whispered back.

"It could have rolled or bounced," Derek whispered.

She thought it was hysterical that they were all whispering like the little Puddy kids in church, but she didn't dare laugh out loud.

"What's so funny?" Jason whispered.

She shook her head. She had to figure out how to get to the wood stove. Was she really going to jump? It might be six feet down. It might be eight feet down. It might be more. Had she ever jumped that far before? She looked up at Derek. She had no reason to think he had attempted such feats, and yet, she did think that. "If I jump down eight feet, will I hurt my legs when I land?"

"It's less than eight feet," Emma said, noticeably not whispering.

"How do you know that?" Zoe asked.

"Because I can see the stove and I can see your feet."

"Oh! So am I over the stove?" Why hadn't she thought to ask her that earlier?

"Yeah. I thought you knew that already."

"How's Levi doing?" Zoe asked.

"Not great. I'm holding him, trying to warm him up, but he's really wet and cold."

Shoot. She had to do this. "All right. Hang on, both of you."

"Bend your knees," Derek said. "Let them cushion the landing. And look around as you drop. If you do start to fall, try to fall in the safest direction, and keep your arms around your head."

"What?" Jason said. "Why? Shouldn't she break her fall with her arms?"

"Definitely not. The arms will protect the head. Do it, Zoe. Time's a wastin'."

She looked into the hole. She had to do this. She swallowed and told her feet to jump.

Searching

They didn't move. She looked down at them in horror. Oh no. *I have to do this,* she told herself. *I volunteered. I can't wuss out now. Everyone is watching.* The whole world would hear this story. Well, not the *whole* world, but *her* whole world.

Chapter 46
Zoe

Jump, she told her legs—but they didn't move.

"What are you waiting for?" Emma asked. "Do you want me to try to come catch you?"

Yes, actually. That sounded like a great idea. But she didn't want to hurt Emma, and she didn't want to make Emma and her body heat leave Levi. For the first time in weeks, Zoe wished she had some alcohol. She was so much braver when she was on the sauce—fearless, actually. This realization made her angry. She shouldn't need booze to make her brave.

Her brain was the problem, not her heart, and certainly not her legs. *God, please help me do this. And help me to land.*

She pushed off the wall and jumped, and this time, her feet left the floor. She started to close her eyes but then remembered what Derek had said: look for a safe landing. But everything she looked at was dark, and then her feet hit, and she'd forgotten to bend her knees.

Emma cried out in celebration as the stove beneath Zoe's feet wobbled perilously. With no idea what she was jumping into, Zoe jumped off the stove. Her feet met the ground earlier than she expected, sending a shock up her spine. There was no pain, though. *Thank you, God.* Now she only needed to get back out of the basement. She was certain this would be easier than getting in. "Say something, Emma. I can't see you."

"Really? I can see you. What, are you guys all deaf *and* blind?"

Zoe started walking toward the sound, and as she went, her eyes adjusted. She *could* see Emma after all. She picked up her speed and then knelt beside Levi. "Hey, Levi."

He didn't respond. She turned and said over her shoulder. "Can you guys get onto that lip?"

"Already on our way," Jason said. "We wanted to make sure you didn't die before we bothered." He was trying to be funny, but he sounded nervous.

"All right," she said more quietly, to Emma. "Let's see if we can get him up." Her eyes fell on his ankle, and she gasped. "Oh wow, that doesn't look good."

"No. That has to be broken, right?"

"Oh yeah. That is very, very broken. We've got to be careful not to let him put any weight on it." She scooched closer. "And not to touch it at all, or let it touch anything." Her stomach churned at the thought of how much pain he was in. "Okay, Levi, we're going to try to move—"

A terrible creaking sound interrupted her, and both she and Emma looked toward the stove as Jason cried out. His foot dangled through the hole but then slowly slid back up out of sight.

"Are you okay?" Emma cried before Zoe could.

"Yeah, yeah. Some of the floor gave way. Guess I weigh more than Zoe."

"He didn't need to sound so surprised," Zoe said.

"We need to hurry." Emma was scared. "I don't know how close to dying he is." She looked down at Levi and put her hand on the top of his head. "Sorry, Levi. Not trying to scare you. Just want to get you out of here."

He didn't respond. He looked almost peaceful lying there, the top of him resting on Emma's body.

"New plan," Derek called out. "We'll go get help. We'll be right back."

"No!" Emma cried with primal fear.

Zoe assumed that she didn't want to be left in this terrifying basement in the dark.

"I don't know how long he'll last. You guys, he's really *really* cold. We need to get him out of here!" There was a startling amount of force in her words, and the men fell silent for a minute.

"All right, then I'll try to pull him up by myself," Jason said. "Maybe the floor will hold if Derek doesn't come with me."

"Why don't you go that way, instead?" Derek said. "I'll stay back here and hold your feet."

"Good idea. Okay, girls, give us a second to get situated."

Zoe watched Jason's feet edging in the wrong direction. What was he doing? Why was he going back? But only a minute later, she saw Jason squirming along on his belly. If the floor gave way now, he was going to do a belly flop into the basement. She wasn't sure this was the best plan, but she bit her tongue. At least his weight was distributed more widely now. She looked at Emma. "He's breathing, right?"

Emma nodded wildly. "Slowly, but yeah."

"Have you checked his pulse?"

Emma shook her head. "Don't know how."

Zoe scooted around to get to his wrist. At first, she couldn't feel any pulse at all, but if he was breathing, didn't that mean that his heart was beating? Why was she even doing this? She had no idea what to do with the information she would glean. *Because you need to do something*, a little voice whispered, and then she found the pulse. She was no expert, but she thought his pulse felt slow and weak. She put the back of her hand to his cheek. It was ice cold.

"Okay, how's this?" Jason called through the hole.

Zoe turned to see his head sticking out over the hole, his arms dangling down into it. He'd abandoned the lip along the wall and had instead laid across rotten, broken boards.

"Please tell me that Derek has a hold of your feet."

"He does."

Jason wasn't quite over the wood stove. Close, but not quite.

"Can you pull him up with your arms alone?" Zoe hated to doubt her Jason, and she hated even more to doubt him aloud, but what he was intending to do didn't seem possible. Pull Levi up at an angle with only his arms?

"I have no idea, but I've been lifting weights three times a week for years. I thought I was doing that for my jump shot, but apparently not. Apparently, I was doing it for this. Come

Searching

on. You two should have already been moving him this way."

"Well excuse us," Zoe said, getting up. "No one told us that." She felt cobwebs hit her head and suppressed a shriek. How big of a threat were cobwebs really, under the circumstances? She looked down at her classmate. "All right, Levi. We're going to try to move you. I'm so, so sorry." She reached down and slid her forearms under his armpits. And then she lifted, grunting as she did so. He was heavier than she'd expected.

He cried out in pain; the noise was deafening in the relative quiet.

"Oh no!" Emma cried at the same time as Zoe cried, "Help me, Emma!"

Chapter 47
Zoe

Emma scrambled to her feet and jammed her petite frame under Levi's armpit. She squiggled to adjust her body, and then she had his arm around her shoulders. Zoe wasn't sure, but she thought Levi had helped make that happen. Zoe moved her own body to his side and got his arm over her shoulder, pleased that Levi was almost as tall as her.

"All right, here we go." Zoe tried to sound chipper, which didn't come naturally. "Levi, don't you dare put that foot on the ground." Oh great, now she sounded like a power-thirsty vice principal.

Levi bent his knee and lifted his ankle a few inches off the ground. Yes, he was definitely helping. That was great news. He was with it a little, anyway. Zoe stepped forward, and nobody came with her. "Come on, Emma!"

"I'm trying!" Emma cried.

Levi put his good foot down on the ground, and the load lightened. Emma caught up to Zoe.

"Okay. Now we go one more step. Levi, on three, try to hop. I promise not to drop you." She didn't know if she could keep this promise, but she would die trying. "One, two, three!" On three, she stepped forward, as did Emma. Levi did try, but his hop fell short, and she and Emma staggered backward—so far backward that she didn't know if they'd made any forward progress at all.

"You guys okay?" Jason shined his flashlight down on them.

"Yes, and get that light out of my face." This time Zoe didn't even feel guilty snapping at him; she was too focused on the weight of the injured human being hanging off her shoulder.

"Maybe you shouldn't be holding the light," Derek said. "If you drop it, we don't have a light." There was a pause. "Don't put it there, you imbecile! It's even more likely to fall!"

"If it falls, Zoe will just pick it up!" Jason said.

Oh awesome. Now she was getting assigned rescue tasks. "You guys need to shut up and let us focus!"

"Yes, ma'am," Derek said.

"Ready, you two?" Zoe took a deep breath.

Levi didn't answer.

"Emma, take a smaller step this time. Ready? One, two, three." Whether Levi was ready or not, the girls stepped forward, and though he didn't have the strength to hold his head up off his chest, he managed to hop.

Zoe was impressed. He was a fighter. She didn't know how he'd gotten himself into this mess, but she admired how hard he was fighting to get out of it.

"Okay, again. One, two, three!" This was the smoothest step yet, and relief flooded Zoe's chest. Don't be relieved yet, she told herself. It was still a long way to that stove. "And again. One, two, three!"

"Awesome, you—" Jason tried.

Zoe didn't let him finish before counting again. One more step, successful. Her foot splashed down into a puddle, but she barely noticed. One-two-three, and another step. Levi cried out in pain. Zoe flinched, but then thought it was a good sign that he was making noise. "Good job, Levi," she said softly. "We're almost there." This wasn't exactly true. They still had over ten feet to go, but she was confident they would do it, one step at a time.

And then they did. They reached the stove, and Emma cried out in relief.

"Hey, Levi," Jason said. "I've talked to your mom. She's back at the church praying. You're going to be okay. And she's going to be so excited to see you."

Levi lifted his head to look at Jason, and they all held their breath. But Levi only let his head fall back to his chest.

For the first time, Zoe wondered how she was going to get Levi onto the stove. "Emma? Can you keep him standing for just a minute?"

Emma looked doubtful.

"Just for a few seconds. I need to climb onto the stove."

"Can't he just lean on the stove?"

Oh yeah. That idea wasn't half bad. Might be good to give Emma a break. "I don't know. Can you, Levi?" As she asked, she took his arm from behind her neck. He wobbled a bit, but Emma shifted her feet, and he stayed upright. Quickly but gently, Zoe placed his hand on the stove in front of him. "This is a solid wood stove. It's not going anywhere. You can lean on it."

On his own, Levi pulled his right arm from around Emma and put it beside his left. He was breathing harder now. Zoe didn't know what this meant.

Zoe scrambled up onto the stove. Then she squatted down and put her arms under his armpits. She did not know if this was going to work. She didn't know if she could do this. Slowly, she pushed herself to a stand, pulling with all she had. Levi screamed in pain, right in her face, and for a second she thought she was going to drop him, but then Emma grabbed his good leg and pushed. Then he came with such force that Zoe almost fell back off the other side of the stove.

He wobbled, and she widened her stance to steady him, her arms wrapped tightly around his waist. He stopped wobbling, and she looked up. "Okay, I've got him on the stove. Now what?"

Jason's arms dangled through the hole, right at eye level. "If he lifts his arms up, I can grab them."

"You're gonna pull him by his arms?"

"Yeah," Jason said, not sounding sure. "At the same time, you'll be pushing, though."

Zoe didn't know what it was, but something about this idea was deeply unsettling.

"Do it," Levi said weakly, and then he slowly lifted his arms above his head. One of them didn't make it and fell to his side, but he took a deep breath and tried again. Zoe could feel him straining.

"You'll pull his arms out of their sockets," Zoe said.

"Okay," Levi said. "Do it." The same arm started to slide down again, but Zoe grabbed it and held it over his head.

Searching

"He's ahead of you a little, not right above you." She pointed his arms in the right direction.

Jason scooted ahead even further, and the floor creaked beneath him. He reached out with one hand and grabbed one of Levi's arms. Then he reached out and grabbed the other. "I've got you, buddy. We're almost out of this rotten house."

Weakly, Levi said, "Pull."

"Push, Zoe!" Jason grunted as he pulled, and Zoe squatted to get her shoulder under Levi's rump.

Again, he cried out in pain.

Zoe stood, her legs shaking under the weight. She so wished she could push straight up. This angle was killing her. But she could feel Levi moving upward, and she pushed even harder to make that keep happening.

"Yah!" Jason cried.

She didn't know what that meant, but it emboldened her, and she cried out with effort.

"Grab hold of me!" Jason cried.

Me? Zoe wondered, and then she was standing straight up, and most of Levi's weight was gone. Jason had taken it. She pushed on Levi's good leg, which was soaked, and she looked up to see Jason had rolled over, and now had Levi's head on his stomach.

"Pull us, Derek!"

And then Zoe saw Jason sliding away, and Levi's legs were lifted out of the hole. Oh wow. They'd actually done it. She looked at Emma and giggled. She bent over and put her hands on her knees, suddenly exhausted.

"We're still in the basement," Emma said.

Chapter 48
Zoe

Zoe stood up straight, and her back cracked. How much had she just strained herself pushing a teenage boy up out of a basement? She looked at Emma, who looked scared. "It's okay. *We're* okay. I'm so glad that Levi is *out* of the basement that I don't mind living here."

"Well, I do! They're going to pull us up too, right?"

Zoe wiped the sweat off her upper lip and nodded. "You don't need them." She squatted down. "Get on my shoulders."

Emma looked doubtful. "Are you serious?"

"Yes. I'm serious. You're a shrimp. If I wasn't already so tired, I could throw you through the hole. Now do it. I want to get out of here too. I was kidding about the living here part."

"I'm not a shrimp." Still looking tentative, Emma climbed onto the stove and grabbed Zoe's shoulder. Zoe offered her a hand, which Emma quickly grasped.

"Come on, don't be shy," Zoe said.

Emma giggled and then swung her right leg over Zoe's shoulder.

"Good. I got you. The other leg now."

A shadow was cast over them. Zoe looked up to see that Jason had reappeared.

"Wow, look at you guys."

Zoe didn't need to hold tightly to Emma's hand—Emma had her in a vice grip. Slowly, Zoe stood to her feet. This shrimp was heavier than she looked.

"Good grief, you are strong," Jason said. His voice was full of admiration, but Zoe wasn't flattered. She didn't want him admiring her for her brute strength. "Are you sure you don't want to play basketball?"

"Really, Jason?" Her voice sounded strained. "Now?"

He chuckled, and Zoe felt him grab Emma. "I got you, kid."

"I'm not a kid," Emma said, grunting.

"You can step on my shoulder, Emma. Use it to push off."

"Really?" Emma asked even as she did just that. Her wet shoe ground into Zoe's shoulder bone, but it only hurt a little. And then Emma was gone, up and out of the hole, just like that. Zoe let out a long breath, feeling mightily accomplished. Then she looked around her surroundings, which wasn't easy with the limited light coming through that hole.

Wait. Why was she so happy, exactly? Sure, she'd helped rescue Levi and helped get Emma out of the basement, but now what? She was still in the basement, and there was no other Zoe to help push her out. Her heart thumped faster, and she tried to reel in that panic.

Jason reappeared. "Okay, now what's the plan?"

"Not sure," Zoe admitted.

"I can try to pull you up, but without you pushing, I'm not sure I can do it." She knew this already. She didn't need to be told. Also, what number weight-comment was this? She'd lost count.

She looked around the basement. "Give me your light."

Only semi-reluctantly, Jason handed his phone down. She shined it around the basement. There was an ancient five-gallon bucket. She could flip that over. That would give her a few feet. But would it be enough? She saw a second five-gallon bucket. It occurred to her to stack them, but she thought that might be a recipe for disaster. Then her eyes landed on a third bucket. First, what was with all the buckets? Second, could she build a pyramid? She hopped down to grab them.

"Where are you going?"

"I'll be right back."

"Hurry. Levi doesn't look so good."

What did he think she was doing, taking some time for some interior decorating? She grabbed one of the buckets and was delighted to find that the bucket was actually two buckets stuck together. She headed back toward the stove, trying to pull them apart on the way. Of course, she couldn't. She handed them up to Jason. "Pull these apart, would you?"

He grabbed them. "No, you can't stack these."

Annoyed, she jumped down again to grab the others. When she returned with two more slimy buckets, Jason had disappeared. Awesome. "Jason?" she said, and then was embarrassed by how panicky she sounded.

He reappeared. "I couldn't pull them apart while dangling into a hole, Zoe." He handed one down to her, which she took wordlessly. Then she built a three-bucket pyramid.

"Oh, like a cheerleader pyramid!" Jason said excitedly.

Zoe pictured a stack of cheerleaders there in front of her and almost laughed. Yes, she would love to step on some skimpy uniforms on her way out of this dungeon. She took the fourth bucket from Jason's dangling hand and placed it front of the pyramid for a step. She

Searching

reached up. "Grab me, will ya? In case this doesn't go as planned."

Jason removed the light from the situation and then reached back into the hole and groped around for her hand. He found it, and electricity exploded down her arm all the way to her shoulder. She couldn't believe that even under the circumstances, he still had that effect on her. She stepped onto the extra bucket and then before she could hesitate, stepped onto the top of the pyramid. It made a discouraging cracking sound, to which she answered, "Pull!" She pushed off like she was in a one-legged jumping championship and waved her free hand around, searching for something to grab onto. It found Jason's other arm, and he dug his fingers into the slippery armpit of her raincoat.

"Pull!" he cried, and at first she thought he meant her, but then she felt someone pulling him, and he started to slide. She hated this feeling: dangling in the air, completely out of control, completely dependent on someone else to make sure she didn't die.

Her head had just popped out of the hole when she stopped moving. They were still pulling, but she was stuck. "Wait!" she cried. The hood of her coat was snagged on one of the broken boards. They didn't wait, didn't stop pulling, and she cried, "Stop!"

They stopped. "Why?" Derek cried, sounding exasperated.

"I'm caught on something."

"Don't let go of me!" Jason's voice made it clear he was straining.

"I have to! I have to free the jacket! And I might be able to pull myself up from here." She had no idea if this was true.

The hand that held her armpit tightened its grip. The other hand let go, and she thought he was going to allow her to try to free herself, but before she could even start, that arm wrapped around her back as he yelled, "Pull!"

Derek pulled, and her body jerked upward. She opened her mouth to protest, but then she heard a weird *crack*, and she lurched forward. And then she was sliding. Jason had tried to flop over onto his back, and now lay awkwardly on his side. He threw his arm around her waist and pulled her the rest of the way out of the hole as Derek pulled him across the floor. This last part seemed so easy that it made the previous struggle seem distant, like a bad dream fading fast.

"Okay, I got it."

Jason let go of her, and she slithered across the floor toward Derek. Derek let go of

Searching

Jason, and he too started working his way, feet first, toward the door. When Zoe reached unbroken floor, she rolled over and sat up, panting.

"Come on, sport," Derek said. "Levi needs to move."

Slowly Jason came to a stand and then held out a hand to Zoe. Zoe accepted his help and came to a stand on violently shaking legs. She was going to be *so sore* tomorrow. She stepped out onto the porch, where Levi lay. Why had they left him out here in the rain?

Derek sensed her question. "Didn't want him to fall through the floor again and thought he might be thirsty."

Well, his thirst might be quenched, but he was also drenched. "Jason, help me get him into the car," she said because she didn't feel comfortable bossing Derek around.

But Derek went to Levi and wrapped his arms under Levi's shoulders. She started to grab Levi's feet, but then remembered his ankle. She stepped forward and hooked one arm under each knee. Then they started toward the car.

Jason ran by them. "I'll start the car." He did, and then he came trotting back to help, but they had him. Derek headed straight for the backseat, and Jason hurried to open the door for them. "Emma! Can you get in the back on the other side, and help us slide him across the seat?"

Emma ran to the car and got in as Derek was placing Levi's torso into the car. He immediately flopped backward, and Emma sort of caught him. Then she pulled him across the seat, climbing back out of the car in the process. "Okay," she said with one hand on his back. "I'm going to close the door and then you can lean on it."

Was Levi even conscious?

Emma yanked her hand away and shut the door before Levi could fall out of the car. And just like that, all of him was in the car—even his badly broken ankle.

Chapter 49
Levi

Levi didn't know if he was dreaming. It felt like it. But if this was a dream, it was a cruel one. He was being rescued. He was being rescued by Jason DeGrave of all people, who hadn't spoken to him since third grade, by the new goth girl, and by some little kid. That didn't make sense. What would Jason DeGrave be doing out in the woods with these two? This made him think it was a dream. And then he kept hearing a fourth voice, which kept singing "Grandma Got Run Over by a Reindeer." This also made him think he was dreaming.

But could he be feeling this much pain in a dream? Maybe the pain was real, and the dream was the way his mind was explaining it. And if that was the case, then the pain had become much worse—worse than it had been since he'd first come to in the cellar. Every bone in his body must be broken. And his head was broken too. It pounded and pounded like a heartbeat, and the pain made his stomach insist on throwing up, but he didn't have the energy.

He didn't have the energy to do anything. He couldn't even open his eyes. Was this what dying felt like? *Okay, God, if this is it, please help me to be brave. And please clear my mind. I don't want to die while some dream or hallucination sings me bad Christmas songs.*

Wait, was he getting *warmer*? Yes, yes he was. Did this mean death? Or was this just another hallucination? He tried to concentrate, tried to order his thoughts, but they refused to cooperate. His mother was praying. He knew that. *God, comfort her. Tell her I'm brave. It's okay.*

Something was different, though. His surroundings felt different. Dryer. And he couldn't hear the water. He remembered being lifted then. Oh yeah, he'd been moved. They'd moved him.

Or had they?

He tried to move his hand to feel around, but he could only wiggle his fingers. But he could definitely tell that he was getting warmer. He tried to open his eyes, but he couldn't. Then he realized he was hearing a new sound.

There was an engine running. Right beside him.

Chapter 50
Zoe

"I am not leaving you girls out here alone," Jason insisted.

He didn't want to leave either or both of them in the woods. But it was also implied that he didn't want to leave either or both of them alone with Derek. Zoe didn't know if this was founded, but to argue would be to call attention to it, and she didn't want to do that to Derek. Maybe he didn't know how Jason felt about that idea.

Or maybe he did. Because he hadn't offered to stay behind to babysit either of them.

"Fine," Derek said. "I'll drive."

It seemed Jason was speechless.

"I'll go with him," Zoe's lips had offered before her brain caught up.

Jason looked at her, worry etched on his forehead.

"Then you can stay here with Emma. The second we have a signal, we'll call for help, and someone will be here to get you."

Jason was still speechless.

"Come on, Derek." She started toward the car, silently cursing her mother for never letting her take Driver's Ed.

"Wait." Jason had found his tongue. "How can you call for help with no phone?"

Oh no. That was a good question. She turned back. "Okay, then, we'll stop at the first house and ask them to call for help."

Jason hesitated and then headed toward her. "No." He held his phone out to her. "You need it more than I do."

She didn't take it. She didn't know who needed it more.

He shook it at her. "Take it. My arm's too tired to stand here holding it out to you."

She took it, and he walked up the slope backward until he stood beside Emma again. Then he took her hand. "We'll be fine. Really. Just hurry."

Emma looked up at him. "Right. We've been through one war together already."

"Right," Jason said.

This wasn't the first time Zoe had heard this war mentioned, and she still didn't know what it was. But right now, she didn't have time to care. "Okay, Derek, let's go. And don't crash us into a tree. We ain't got no time for that." She was trying to be funny, but she didn't hear any laughter.

She climbed into the front seat and looked back to make sure Levi was still okay, though okay was relative right now.

"Whoa," Derek said as he shut the door behind him. "It's too warm in here." He turned down the fan. He put the car in reverse and cut the wheel. "We can't let him warm up too fast." He looked into the rearview. "You doing okay, kid?" He didn't wait for an answer. He stomped on the gas and backed the car up—directly at the woods.

Awesome. Now they were going to get stuck.

Derek stomped on the brake and cut the wheel the other way. Then he pulled back out onto the driveway. Amazingly, they were pointed in the right direction. "Hang on, kid. You're almost out of the woods." Then he started singing "Here Comes Santa Claus."

Zoe tried not to groan. She'd been hoping Levi was conscious, but maybe it would be better if he wasn't.

Levi cried out in pain.

Oh no. She turned around in her seat and tried to see his face, but he was pushed up against the door behind her, and he was all dark shadows. She tried to find his hand, taking care not to touch anything that might be injured. Her fingers found his, which were like ice. She grabbed them and held them gently. "Hang on, Levi." Zoe wrapped her left arm around her headrest to hold herself in place as the bumps jostled her around. "You might need to slow down."

"I'm sorry for his suffering, but pain is a good thing."

She was now beyond annoyed. "No, it's not."

"Pain means he's still alive. I don't know how many injuries he has, but if we don't get him to the hospital, his pain might end prematurely." Derek coughed. "I'm going to try not to let that happen."

Zoe was tempted to blame it on her imagination or on wishful thinking, but she thought she felt Levi's fingers squeeze hers. Then they hit another rock, and Levi cried out again. How long was this godforsaken driveway?

Chapter 51
Nora

Nora had sat with her head bowed for so long that her neck had stiffened. She tipped her head back as she rubbed at the new knot in her neck. Even though she kept her eyes closed, she could see lights through her eyelids—*supernaturally* bright lights. Her eyes popped open to see that she was only looking at the ceiling lights.

This was a crushing disappointment. She hadn't seen the light of God or the light of heaven—only the ceiling lights. Yet that despair that had lifted when she'd first seen them did not return. She waited for it. Waited for the weight to hit her shoulders, for the sickness to return to her stomach, for the panic to return to her chest—but none of that came.

She looked around the circle at all the people praying. Most of them she didn't know. Some of them she'd never even seen before. She'd heard that some of them were from Mattawooptock, but she thought most of them were local people she didn't know—people who didn't know her.

A few of them had tears rolling down their cheeks. Others had their hands in the air. Most of them had prayed aloud, sometimes talking over one another, but for the most part, taking turns. A few of them had prayed complete nonsense. Unless they were speaking a language she didn't know, she thought they'd probably lost their minds. But who was she to criticize? Maybe that type of praying worked. What did she know? She was tempted to scream at God right now.

Esther looked up at her. "What?" she whispered.

Nora shook her head, not understanding what she was asking.

Esther furrowed her brow. "You look different."

Yes, she might. She felt a little different. "I don't know."

"What don't you know?"

"I don't know what's happening. Maybe I've just reached a new level of exhaustion. But I feel different."

"How do you feel?" the exceptionally tall woman beside her asked.

Nora looked over at the woman and was partially distracted by her giant floppy orange hat. "I don't know. I guess I'm less scared." She could feel other eyes on her now. "Like I said, maybe I'm just too tired to be scared anymore." She had another theory, but she didn't want to give voice to it. Maybe part of her was starting to accept that her son wasn't coming home.

"I don't think that's it," Rachel said so seriously that Nora didn't know which theory she was referencing, the spoken or the unspoken one. "Come on, family. Let's amp up this effort!" She held both her arms into the air, and several followed suit. A few went to their knees, and several people started praying aloud at the same time.

A weird energy began to buzz in Nora's chest.

She was scared to recognize what this energy might be. Was it possible? Was it hope? And if so, where was it coming from?

Chapter 52
Zoe

They hit what felt like a boulder, and Zoe cursed.

Derek stopped singing to say, "I don't think your grandmother would appreciate that." Then he started singing again.

Zoe looked over her shoulder out the windshield. "Are we even in the driveway anymore or are you just off-roading?"

The car started to slow, and Zoe thought her criticism had influenced him, but then he turned on the blinker, and she let out a long breath. They'd reached the road. "Do you really need to signal?" she asked as she checked the phone for service. "There's no one around."

"I'm really trying not to break any rules," Derek said and then started singing again. He pulled out onto the road, and Levi whimpered.

"Still no bars, but it shouldn't be long now." She looked back at Levi. "We're on a road now. Should be a smoother ride."

He didn't respond, but he was still breathing.

Derek accelerated, they hit the tiniest bump, and Levi cried out again. Zoe squeezed his fingers. "Almost there." She really hoped the tiny Carver Harbor hospital would have what Levi needed. Or that they could at least make him more comfortable and then keep him alive until they got him to a real hospital. She looked at the phone again. One bar. "Stop!"

Derek didn't stop.

"Stop, Derek! I have a signal!"

"Then call!" he cried.

"I might lose the signal!" she screamed as she dialed 9-1-1. "Stop the car!"

He slowed down and pulled the car over, and she did still have one bar.

"Nine-one-one, what's your emergency?"

"I'm in Carver Harbor. We found the missing kid, and he's in bad shape. He needs an ambulance."

"Where in Carver Harbor?"

Zoe had no idea.

"We are a twenty-minute walk north from The Reef and a ten-minute walk east of the lighthouse," Derek said.

"Which lighthouse?" Zoe whispered.

"I don't know its name. The one with lights."

Thinking it was probably useless, Zoe repeated this information to the operator, all the while trying to figure out a better way to give their location.

"The Reef?" the operator asked.

"It's a bar. We are pretty close to the edge of the peninsula, on the western side of it." She looked out the windshield, desperate for a landmark.

"We're close to the dump," Derek said. "Tell the ambulance to meet us there." He stepped on the gas, and Levi whimpered again.

"No sir, please stay where you are," the operator tried.

"We'll be right at the dump entrance. We'll wait there," Zoe said. "Thank you." She started to hang up.

"Wait! Please stay on the line."

"I can't, sorry." Zoe hung up and dialed her grandmother.

Chapter 53
Esther

After hours of repetition, suddenly everything felt different. There was a desperate charge in the air. It was getting late. People were getting tired. Some of them had left. It was pouring outside.

And Esther couldn't get a hold of Zoe.

All sorts of horror filled her mind. They were lost in the woods. They'd slipped and fallen into the ocean. Their car had broken down. There was a madman kidnapping teenagers, and he'd gotten Zoe too. Derek was a madman after all. One by one, Esther tried to stomp these thoughts out. She silently recited Philippians 4:8 over and over, and then Walter came through the front door and made a beeline for her as if he had news to share. Her breath caught.

He took her hands in his.

"What?" she forced out. "What is it?"

"Are you all right?"

"Am *I* all right?" What kind of a question was that? "Yes, I'm fine. Why, what is it?" she asked again.

"I don't know." Rainwater dripped off his chin, and he wiped it on his wet shoulder without breaking eye contact. "When I came through the door, you looked like you'd seen a ghost." He paused. "You're pale. Here, let's sit down."

"I don't need to sit," she snapped. Then she looked at the prayer circle guiltily. She didn't want to disturb them. She sidestepped away from them. "Sorry. I didn't mean to snap. I'm just worried about the kids. I can't get a hold of Zoe."

"Oh." His brow furrowed. "Do you want me to go look for her?"

She considered it. Then she let out a long breath. "No. We need to focus on Levi," she said as her heart screamed otherwise. She tried to fake it, tried to convince him with her eyes.

He bought it. "All right. We came back to swap maps." He glanced over his shoulder at the map table. "We're running out of peninsula. We'll find him soon."

Or he's not on the peninsula, she thought but didn't say. Then she remembered Nora's change. "I think we're close too. Something's different about Nora. I think God has spoken to her."

"Did she say that?" Walter was a new believer, and his lawyer-brain remained skeptical about a lot of spiritual things.

Searching

"She didn't," Esther admitted, and Walter looked relieved.

"Your phone's ringing."

"Oh?" She hurried back to the prayer circle and bent to snatch it out of her purse. She didn't recognize the number, which usually meant she wouldn't answer the phone, but under the circumstances, she thought she should.

"Hello?" she said tentatively.

"Gramma! We found him! Tell his mom, we found him!"

Esther didn't hesitate. It was as if her mouth had a mind of its own. "They've found him!" she hollered, louder than she'd hollered in years. Then she went back to the phone, as dozens of people flooded toward her, all asking questions at the same time. "Where are you, honey? Is he okay? Are you okay?"

"He's hurt really bad. We're on our way to the dump, and we—"

"The dump?" Esther cried.

"He was at the dump?" someone echoed.

Walter tried to push the crowd back away from Esther. "Give her a second. She's finding out."

When Esther heard Walter say this, she had a sharp realization. "Let Nora through."

No one had to work hard to make this happen. Nora was already pushing her way to the front. As she did so, Walter planted a big old kiss right on Esther's lips. She couldn't believe it. She looked at him wide-eyed, silently asking, "What was that?"

He shrugged, his smile as broad as a barn. "I couldn't help it. I'm just so happy. Thought we should celebrate."

Nora made it to Esther and looked at her pleadingly.

"Zoe, honey? Are you near to Levi? Can you give him the phone?"

"He's right here. I don't think he can talk, but I'll hold the phone up to his ear."

Chapter 54
Zoe

Zoe put the phone on speaker and then slowly spun around in her seat until she was on her knees, with her head cocked off to the side. She held the phone in front of Levi. "Someone wants to talk to you."

"Levi!" his mother screamed, and Zoe hurried to turn the volume down.

"He's right here, Mrs. Langford," Zoe said softly. "I don't think he can talk, but he's conscious."

"Levi, baby, I love you so much …"

Zoe could hear a million tears in her voice. Maybe more.

"Thank you for hanging on, baby. I knew you would make it. You are so strong. I am so proud of you, and so, so excited to see you. Just keep hanging on, okay? Did you guys call an ambulance?" she asked, obviously talking to Zoe.

Zoe, who, seconds ago, had felt as if she were trampling on some private moment, quickly said. "Yes, they're meeting us at the dump. That was the only close place we could think of. And I'm sure they will take him to the hospital. His ankle is definitely broken, and I think …" Zoe wasn't sure how to say what she was trying to say. She didn't want to scare his mother any more.

"You think what?"

"I have no idea. It's just, he's okay. I know he's going to be okay. I can tell, but there's more wrong with him than the ankle. I think maybe he got too cold or too hungry or something."

"Mum," Levi whispered so quietly that Zoe almost missed it.

"He just said, 'Mom'!"

The woman on the other end of the line sobbed.

"I'll put the phone closer to his mouth." Zoe moved the phone, but Levi didn't say anything else, and then Derek was pulling over. Zoe looked out the window to see the closed gate of the dump. "We're here, Levi. No more moving around until you're in the ambulance moving around."

He didn't respond, and she looked at his chest to make sure it was still rising and falling.

It was. Slowly, but it was moving.

"I'll be right there," Mrs. Langford said.

"Actually, by the time you get here, we might have left. You might want to go straight to the hospital."

Searching

"I'll be right there. You hang on, Levi!"

Zoe heard her try to give the phone back to Esther, heard Esther tell her to take it, and then Mrs. Langford said, "Okay, I'm going to try to keep you on the line. But I'm coming. You just hang on, baby."

"Let me give you a ride," a male voice said. Gramma's sweetie, Zoe thought.

Then her grandmother said. "Yes, I'll come too." And Zoe's heart leapt at these words. Levi was definitely the center of attention here, but she'd had a long, hard night too, and she wanted her Gramma.

"Gramma, wait!" she cried.

"What?" Nora sounded panicked. "What is it?"

"No, no, Levi's okay. But someone needs to go up ..." She looked at Derek. "What is the name of that stupid road?"

"Chitwood Road," Derek provided.

She repeated the name. "A few miles up there, there's an overgrown driveway. It's pretty long, but at the end of it is Jason and Emma. Someone needs to go get them." She listened while Mrs. Langford repeated this.

Then she heard her grandmother say, "You left them in the woods?"

"We had to," she started to explain, but then she saw headlights. At first she thought it was the ambulance, but they were coming from the wrong direction, and there were no red lights or sirens. Whatever it was, it was big. The vehicle slid in alongside their tiny car.

It was an SUV.

"I don't know whose it is, but it was at the church." Derek sounded relieved. Maybe he'd been worried about getting caught behind the wheel.

Two doors flew open, and two people spilled out. And then two more. And two more came around from the other side. What was this, a clown car? She recognized Emma first, and breath rushed out of her. "Never mind. Someone found them."

A man leaned on the car and smiled in at them. Zoe didn't recognize him.

Derek rolled the window down. "Did I do something wrong, officer?"

Zoe didn't know if he was making a joke or if he'd gotten his wires crossed.

"How's he doing?" Emma asked through the window.

Zoe ducked down, trying to see out the window, trying to make sure Jason was with them.

"Jason's here," Emma said, and Zoe was glad it was dark, because her cheeks were red. Then Derek flung his door open, and they

Searching

were bathed with a blinding light. She glanced at Levi, but he didn't seem to notice.

"The ambulance is on its way," Zoe told her.

Emma slid into the front seat, which, Zoe was pretty sure, wasn't why Derek had vacated it.

"How did you get here?"

"Galen found us."

"Who's Galen?"

"The Mattawooptock pastor."

"He just happened to be wandering around out there?"

Emma shrugged. "We were in his map."

Zoe sighed and rested her head on the headrest. "Wow, so someone would have found him soon even if we didn't."

"We don't know how long he had," Emma said quietly. "I'm glad we found him when we did. And they might not have thought to look in the basement." She folded her pink hands in her lap. "I think it all happened the way it was supposed to happen."

Zoe had her doubts that Levi was ever *supposed* to go into that house or fall into that basement, but she didn't want to argue with Emma.

Another car pulled into the small gravel area. Still not an ambulance.

A face she recognized to be a cop came into view. Somehow he determined that this mysterious Galen was the man in charge and offered his hand, introducing himself as Officer Carl Pettiford of the Carver Harbor PD. Then he bent down and looked in at Levi. Zoe was startled at how sad he looked. Shouldn't he be thrilled? They'd found the missing kid!

Chapter 55
Nora

The ambulance did beat them to the dump, but it hadn't left yet. Nora didn't wait for the wheels to stop turning before she was climbing out of the car and running toward the small car the DeGrave kid drove. What a miracle that kid had turned out to be. She remembered when she'd first stopped him to ask for his help. She'd felt so foolish. But what a great decision that had been.

Maybe it hadn't been a coincidence. Maybe God knew that this was how Levi needed to get found. She didn't know, and she didn't need to know right now.

They had her son on a stretcher. She ran toward them. One of the paramedics tried to stop her, but the one strapping him into place recognized her from work. "It's okay. That's his mom."

She grabbed Levi's hand and burst into tears. "Oh my baby." She waited for something to change on his face, but there was nothing. No movement, no expression. Certainly no words.

"He's unconscious, ma'am, but don't worry. We're going to do everything we can."

These words sent a chill cascading over her shoulders. "Is he going to make it?"

They started toward the ambulance. She walked alongside, waiting for an answer, but one didn't come. Panic gripped her. No way would God bring them this far just to let Levi die. He wouldn't do that, right? *Please, God. Anything. I'll give you anything.*

"Ma'am?"

She looked over her shoulder and into the sincere eyes of the Mattawooptock pastor. "They're trained not to answer these questions. They're not allowed to. But it doesn't mean he won't be just fine."

"Yeah," a tall girl with short, black hair chimed in. "He was conscious just a little bit ago."

They hoisted him into the ambulance.

"Can I ride along?"

The paramedics exchanged a look, and one of them nodded. "Sure. Hop in." He gave her a hand, and she slid onto the warm, dry bench beside Levi. She was grateful for the warmth. She hadn't realized how wet she'd gotten in just a few minutes outside. She looked at her son. He was drenched. His lips were blue.

The paramedic was cutting through his coat. At first this scared her, but then she realized he was likely getting ready to put an IV in. The bus lurched forward, and then they were underway with sirens blaring.

"He looks so cold. Can I cover him up?"

The man across from her nodded and pointed with this chin. "Right there."

She turned and found a few blankets folded up neatly on a shelf. She pulled one of them out and then shook it out. Then she gently laid it on her son. The blanket wouldn't reach from his toes to his chin, so she opted to cover his feet. She couldn't believe how big he was. She clearly remembered snippets of the day he was born. It had been a difficult delivery, but when she'd looked down at that chubby little face, she had known that it had been worth all the pain. Back then, this new kind of love had gripped her with such intensity she had wondered how anyone could survive it. She could remember thinking that what she was feeling was a maximum love. An infinite love. There was no love in the world stronger or greater than that love she'd felt that first day she saw his face. She'd known then that she would do anything to care for, to love, to protect that boy.

And the love she felt right now in this ambulance was even stronger. How was that possible? She didn't know. But it was there.

Chapter 56
Levi

Levi woke to the disorienting combination of an incredible amount of pain and a euphoria. He looked around the room, a hospital room. His mom sat beside him with her head beside his hip, snoring softly. He wanted to talk to her, tell her about what had happened to him, thank her for making sure people were looking for him, thank her for being such an awesome mother, apologize for the times he'd been rotten—but he didn't want to wake her up.

Soft light spilled through a window he couldn't quite see out of. It was daylight. How had he gotten here? He had fragments of memories in his brain, but they didn't fit together into anything that made sense. He remembered falling. He remembered the basement so clearly it was as if it was a part of him now. He remembered their voices. He remembered them helping him across the cellar, telling him to hop. The idea of hopping seemed so impossible now, but he thought he'd done it. He remembered Jason pulling him out of the basement. He remembered lying on the ground with the rain dripping on his face; it had been so cold, but he hadn't cared because he'd been so happy to be free of that house.

And he remembered Gamp. He remembered things that Gamp had said: They're coming ... The grave had no victory over me ... God searches the heart. He'd been right about the first thing; had he also been right about the rest? He remembered praying, really praying, pleading and begging with God. Had that done something? He'd felt that need, that need for rescue, that need for God, *so* strongly in that basement, but that feeling was fading fast. God wasn't real, was he? That was just how he'd gotten through the ordeal.

His mother stirred. Again he wanted to wake her and again he didn't.

But this time she woke on her own, slowly sitting up. She didn't let go of his hand, and her free hand went to the back of her neck, where she rubbed. She opened her eyes and squinted as she focused. Then she made eye contact with him and she let out the cutest little squeal. His face spread into a grin so quickly that it hurt his cheeks.

"My baby!" She jumped up, leaned over him, and grabbed his sore cheeks with both hands. Then she started kissing him repeatedly on his forehead, and he felt her hot tears on his head.

Slowly, he reached up and wrapped his fingers around her wrist. "Mom," he said, and he couldn't believe how raspy his voice was.

She let go of him and slid away. "I'm sorry. Did I hurt you?"

He tried to shake his head, but it hurt too much. "No, you didn't."

Smiling like he'd never seen her smile before, she slid the chair even closer to his bed and sat down. Then she took that same hand into both of hers and squeezed. "I can't even tell you what a miracle you are."

Her words hit a tuning fork deep in his memory. She'd used to tell him he was a miracle! When he was little! Wow, she hadn't said that in a long time. Which made sense. Because he'd stopped resembling a miracle quite a while back.

"I love you," he said, and again, couldn't believe the raspiness. He sounded like he'd swallowed Drano. His free hand went to his throat as if checking to make sure it was still there.

"Take it easy with talking. You tried earlier, and the doctor said being hard to talk is normal. You're severely dehydrated, and he said you probably overused your voice trying to call for help."

Had he? Had he screamed for help? He couldn't remember. Guess God wants me to be quiet for a while, he thought, and mentally jumped. There was God again. "I have so much to say," he tried, but she shushed him.

"We have plenty of time for that."

But they didn't, did they? He was going to work much harder at living to a ripe old age, but he didn't know how much time he had left. "I'm sorry." An embarrassing tear leaked out of the corner of his eye.

Her eyes filled with tears as she reached out to wipe his away. "I know, baby."

He closed his eyes, exhausted. "I didn't mean to."

"I know. Those kids, the kids who found you? They've told the cops all about Kendall, and Kendall told the cops all about Shane. So they're not getting away with what they did to you."

"They didn't do anything."

"Yes, they did."

"No." He tried to swallow, but his mouth was dry. Dehydrated indeed. "I did it to myself. And I'm sorry. I'm sorry for everything. For the last ..." He tried to do some mental math. "Six years or so."

She laughed, and it was music to his heart. "It's okay. Nobody is perfect. I certainly haven't been. But we've gone through some hard things, and we survived." She squeezed his hand again. "Baby, no matter what has happened, no matter what trouble you've found, I want you to know that I am so, so, so proud of you. I was so scared that I was never going to see you again and not be able to tell you that. I am so proud to call you my son, and I wouldn't trade you for any other son in the world."

Her words took his breath away. Did she really feel that way? About him? That was insane! He was a dud!

She must have read his doubt because she added, "You are so strong and so brave. You have always been confident enough to be yourself, and I admire that so much. And you are so, so stubborn." She laughed and brushed some tears off her cheek with the back of her hand. "I've sometimes hated that, but I don't think I'll ever hate it again. Being stubborn is what kept you alive up there." She smiled and gazed at him. "You are so *tough*, and you're going to make such a good man. Sorry. Correction. You are *already* a good man."

Except that he wasn't, and he knew that. "Mom, there's something else I need to tell you."

Chapter 57
Levi

Levi searched his brain for words, words that wouldn't make him sound insane. "I saw Gamp." Shoot. That had totally sounded insane.

His mother leaned back in her chair a little. "What?" she said softly.

He tried to shrug, but his shoulders didn't obey him. "I don't know if he was real or ..." His voice gave out. He weakly pointed at a pitcher of water on a nearby table, and she leapt up to pour him some. Then she put the straw into his mouth like he was a baby. He would've laughed if he wasn't so focused on the water. It hurt to swallow, but the water felt miraculous sliding down his throat. And he could feel it as it kept going, all the way down through his stomach. It almost tickled. He nodded to let her know that she could take the straw away. "Thank you." He wiped his mouth on his sheet. "I don't know if he was real, but I know he wasn't a ghost. Nothing like that. I think maybe God sent him to me to get me through."

Her doubtful expression softened. "Levi, you can't imagine how much I've prayed.

Prayed and prayed and prayed. I read your Gamp's Bible as if your location was hidden in its pages." She closed her eyes and sighed. "I guess, in a way, it was." She opened her eyes again and looked at him. "So who am I to say that God wouldn't send your Gamp to help? Who am I to say ..." Her voice drifted off thoughtfully.

"He helped a lot." Again, Levi struggled to find the right words. "He talked to me about God."

His mother tipped her head to the side and gazed at him. All this gazing was making him self-conscious. "And I'm betting every word was true. Levi, I think—no, I *know*—we've been wrong about God. I think that, at the end of his life, when Gamp was all God-crazy, and we poked fun at him ..." She sighed. "Well, I think he was right."

There was a soft knock on the door, and Levi looked too quickly. A sharp pain shot up the side of his neck.

A man Levi had never seen before stepped through the doorway.

"Hi, Pastor," his mother said.

"Hi, Nora." He smiled broadly at Levi. "Hi, Levi. You don't know me, but I feel as though I know you. Welcome home." He turned his smile to Levi's mother. "I don't want to intrude.

I just wanted to see if you need anything, any help this morning."

His mom seemed to be considering it, which surprised Levi. Normally she was so proud and didn't want to accept charity. "I can't think of anything, no."

"That's probably a good sign. But if you *do* need anything at any time, please don't hesitate to call me or the church, okay?" He turned back to Levi. "And in the meantime, we'll continue to pray for complete healing." He paused, nodded, and turned toward the door. "You guys have a blessed day." And he was gone.

Part of Levi wanted to comment on what a weirdo that guy had been, but that weirdo had left him with a good feeling in his gut. He'd felt like he mattered, like he had value. So, Levi said, "He seems nice."

His mother laughed. "You have no idea. That man doesn't know us from a hole in the wall, and he organized the whole search."

He did? Why?

"To think I almost didn't even go into the church. I only walked in to ask if they'd seen you."

He wasn't quite following. "You were out looking for me?"

"I was. And I was all alone. Until I walked onto that property. Then I had more help than I could handle." She looked him in the eye. "Honey, people came all the way from Mattawooptock."

He'd heard the name, but he had no idea where Mattawooptock was. It blended in his mind with all the other weird Maine towns: Mattawamkeag, Madawaska, Meddybemps ... He couldn't remember them all, and his mental list-building was interrupted by another knock on the door.

This time he looked up to see two police officers come through the door.

His chest tightened in fear. He recognized them both.

"They helped with the search too," his mother whispered.

He relaxed—a little.

"You look a lot better," one of them said. "That's great to see. I'm Officer Pettiford, and this is Officer Monnikendam."

Sounds like a Maine town, Levi thought, and bit the inside of his cheek.

The first one, Pettiford, nodded toward Levi's mom. "That's quite a mother you have there. She wasn't going to let you stay lost for long."

Levi's chest swelled with pride. He did have the best mom ever.

Pettiford flipped open a notepad. "Can you tell us what happened that night?"

Levi swallowed hard. He didn't want to go through all this. "I don't remember much."

There was a beat, and then Pettiford said, "Then tell us what you do remember. Shane has already told us quite a bit. We're just trying to fill in some holes."

Levi didn't know what to do. He didn't want to be a rat, but the idea of lying made his skin crawl. And surprisingly, he felt no anger toward Shane or Kendall. He remained shocked that they'd done what they'd done, but somehow he felt like he was past it. He never intended to spend any time with them again, ever, but neither did he want them to get into trouble. So, leaving out the part about the drugs, he told the story, ending with, "I don't think they meant me harm. I think they were just scared."

Pettiford studied him for an uncomfortably long time and then jotted something down in his notebook.

"What can you tell me about Kendall's relationship with his father?"

What? What did that have to do with anything?

Searching

Pettiford stared at him, waiting for an answer.

Levi wasn't sure how to describe Kendall's father without using words you're not supposed to use when talking to a cop.

"Have you ever heard or seen anything to indicate someone might have abused Kendall?"

Levi grew distinctly uncomfortable.

Pettiford continued to stare at him.

"Kendall never said much, but he did have an occasional shiner. And he didn't speak highly of his dad."

"What does this have to do with anything?" his mother asked.

"Two related cases, ma'am. We're trying to prevent any more fear and suffering." He gave her a stoic nod, looked at Levi one more time, and then flipped his notebook shut. "I sure am glad you're okay, Levi. Let us know if you think of anything else you think we should know."

Levi gave him a small nod. It was all he could manage.

The policemen left the room, and immediately a harried man in a white lab coat ran in.

Levi looked at his mother wide-eyed. "I have never been this popular."

Chapter 58
Levi

"Good morning, young man!" The doctor sounded happier than he looked.

At least Levi assumed he was a doctor. He could be a nurse. Or the cook, for all Levi knew. Whoever he was, he was really excited about the hand sanitizer.

When he'd finished rapidly massaging the goo into his skin, he pulled a clipboard out from under his arm. "All right. Your scans look good. We don't see any skull fracture or bleeding."

Levi looked at his mother. They'd thought he'd fractured his skull?

"Which, frankly, surprises me, given the amount of swelling." The doctor stared at him, and Levi met his eyes. "You are one lucky young man. But you most definitely have a concussion. So! It's important to rest, both physically and mentally, while your brain heals. Not that you're going to be able to do much with that ankle." He chortled. "And even after the surgery, it will take a few days before you'll feel like moving around."

Levi looked at his mother. "Surgery?"

Searching

"Yeah," she said, looking sad. "You ripped your ankle to shreds. They need to pin it back together again."

Absurdly, Levi thought of Humpty Dumpty. And then he suddenly wanted potato chips.

"Nothing to worry about, though. We'll have you shipshape soon. But you'll be right here for the next few days, so get comfortable." The doctor waggled a finger at him. "For now, rest. Really try to relax. No stimulation. Limit your screen time."

The thought of his phone made Levi's chest ache. How good it would be to get his phone back! Where was it now, anyway? Still in Kendall's backseat? The doctor scurried out of the room, and Levi looked at his mother. "I have no idea where my phone is."

She chuckled ruefully. "I found it in a field."

"In a field? Where?"

"Clark Cove Road."

What? Why? That was nowhere near where he'd been. "They threw my phone into some random field?" he said quietly. The more he thought about that, the more it hurt.

His mother nodded sadly.

Levi chuckled. "I guess it's a good thing the cops came to talk to me before I found that out."

"Oh, don't worry. I made sure the cops knew that detail." Her jaw clenched. She hadn't forgiven his friends yet.

Yet another knock at the door. He groaned, thinking they should shut and lock the door. But when he looked up, his heart filled with joy. At first he wasn't even sure who he was looking at and why he was so joyful, but then his tired, wounded brain got the puzzle pieces into some kind of order: he was looking at his rescuers, the "they" his grandfather had promised. He smiled broadly, both excited to see them and suddenly feeling a bit shy.

The girls walked in slowly as if they were feeling a bit shy too.

His mother had hopped up. "Here, have a seat."

None of them sat, though.

Jason DeGrave, never shy, stepped up and held out a hand. "You look great, bud."

Levi accepted his handshake, wondering when they'd become buds. He looked at the girls one at a time. "I don't know your names."

The tall girl said, "Zoe," and the younger girl chirped, "Emma!"

Levi nodded. "I'm not sure how to thank you all." He frowned. "Where's the other guy?" He'd barely finished the sentence before he panicked. *Had* there been another guy? Had

Searching

he imagined the Christmas music? His cheeks got hotter and hotter until he feared they were going to burst into flames.

But then Jason said, "His name is Derek. We don't really know him, and we were going to invite him, but we couldn't find him."

"You don't know where he lives?" his mom asked.

Jason shook his head, looking regretful. "We're going to find that out. How are you feeling?" He seemed in a hurry to change the subject.

"Like I've been run over by a train. Three times."

They all laughed, and much of the nervous tension in the room vanished.

"He's going to be okay, though," his mom hurried to say. "He has a bad concussion and a broken ankle. He was hypothermic and badly dehydrated but is recovering nicely from all that."

Jason nodded sagely.

"You were *so* cold," Emma said. "I was scared you were too cold."

"I was scared of that too," Levi said.

They all held still, awkwardly staring at one another until Zoe said, "Well, we should probably get out of your hair. We just wanted to check on you. Let us know if you need anything. And when you bust out of here, let's do something fun, and like, *wicked* safe."

He laughed. He liked this girl.

"Safe *and* toasty warm," Emma added.

He nodded. "Sounds like a plan."

"Thanks for coming by," his mother said. "And also, you know, for saving my son's life and all."

"You bet," Jason said, as if it had been nothing at all.

Levi couldn't remember clearly, but he had a feeling it hadn't been nothing. He thought he remembered a lot of straining, pulling, and groaning.

Jason and Zoe turned to leave, but Emma stepped up to his bed and tucked something into his hand. "I don't know if this is yours, it looks kind of old, but I found it where you were lying. So just in case I thought—"

"Let me guess ..." Levi glanced at his mother. "A wood carving."

"Yeah!" Emma sounded elated. "So it is yours! Oh, I'm so glad I grabbed it then. I almost didn't."

Without looking at his hand, Levi said, "Let me guess again. It's a dove?"

Emma scowled a little. "I don't think so. I think it's supposed to be a monkey." She smiled again and then turned on her heel and bounced out of the room.

Levi lifted his hand and uncurled his fingers to take a look. Sure enough: that was a monkey.

Chapter 59
Esther

The sanctuary was a mess. Esther had slept most of the day away on Monday, but now it was Tuesday. They had a bean supper tonight, and she needed to get the church put together again. She'd called in reinforcements, but they weren't there yet.

But as she set about picking up the dozens of coffee cups and doughnut wrappers, she heard a scraping sound in the basement. She froze. What was that? She hadn't seen any cars outside. She tiptoed to the top of the stairs, though tiptoeing was a little silly since she'd been stomping around up there for ten minutes already. "Hello?" she called softly.

Adam Lattin appeared at the bottom of the stairs. "Hey, there!" He took the stairs two at a time.

"Careful of that railing; it's wobbly."

"Nah, I fixed it." He came to a halt beside her and eyed the trash bag in her hands. "Come to pick up a bit?"

"We've got a supper here tonight. I came to pick up a lot." Feeling guilty of boasting, she quickly added, "Others will be here soon."

"Oh yeah? Who's coming?"

Searching

She rattled off the usual suspects, "Rachel, Vicky, Barbara, Dawn, Cathy, and Vera. Vera's not really well enough to do much physical work, but we appreciate her spiritual support."

He nodded, looking thoughtful. "And Walter?"

"Walter?" Her cheeks got hot. "What about him?"

"Is he your beau?"

She laughed out loud. "Beau? Are you trying to use old people tongue?"

He laughed too. "Seemed silly to call him a boyfriend when he's in his sixties."

Sixties? Was Adam sure? How did he know that? Was Walter really only in his *sixties*? She forced herself to breathe and tried to keep her cheeks from getting any pinker. She'd been robbing the cradle for weeks, and she hadn't even known it!

Adam waited for an answer.

"Yes, sort of. I suppose. He might be my *beau*."

Adam grinned broadly. "Excellent. I would love to do a wedding."

This was more than her cheeks could bear. She turned away quickly.

"He'll be here shortly. I already called him to help me move the pews."

Esther glanced back.

"I try to be a mighty man of God, but I can't slide pews around by myself."

She scurried away to find something else to do, far away from the new pastor's prying questions and suggestions. Wait. Was he their new pastor? She didn't know. No one had discussed it since the yogurt had hit the fan after church, but surely, after how he had sprung into action, did any of them care that he wasn't the world's most gifted preacher?

Slowly, her friends trickled in, and one by one, she asked them: Don't you think we should hire him?

Rachel: Absolutely.

Dawn: I think so. He's such a cutie pie.

Cathy: If we don't, I don't think God is going to be happy with us.

Barbara: Yes, but we should invite guest preachers often.

Vera: Quickly. I want him to do my funeral.

Vicky: Maybe.

Esther called this unanimous but didn't try to make it official until they had the church put back together. Then, just as Rachel was about to make her escape, Esther cleared her throat. "Could we speak briefly in the upper room?" She caught Walter staring at her and avoided his gaze.

Searching

Hence, she was surprised when he joined them in the upper room, but, she realized, she *hadn't* specified who exactly she was inviting. And it wasn't as if their church was only going to allow for female elders. "I've spoken with each of you ..." Oops. She hadn't asked Walter. "I've asked *most* of you," she corrected, "and I think it's obvious that Adam Lattin is the man for the job. I wanted to officially agree that we invite the congregation to vote on it this Sunday after church."

"Does that mean he's going to preach again on Sunday?" Barbara said, sounding worried.

"We should certainly invite him to," Cathy said.

"And," Walter said, his eyes still on Esther, "if I may, let's tell him the plan. Let's be completely transparent. Let's tell him that we want him, and that all we need is the formal vote."

Esther nodded. "That's a good idea."

"Of course you'd think that," Vicky said.

They all ignored her.

Esther clapped her hands together and stood. "Great. Then I'll see some or all of you back here for the supper."

Everyone stood except for Vicky, who put her petite feet up on the white wicker coffee table. "I'm going to stay right here. Tonya stole my car again."

They all knew that Tonya had done no such thing; not only had Vicky told her that she could use the car whenever she wanted, but Vicky *loved* having Tonya and Emma live with her, using her home and her car. While no one would call Vicky *happy*, exactly, she had been far less unhappy since Tonya and Emma had moved in.

The women filtered out of the room, and Esther started to follow, but Walter touched her arm. "Might I have a moment?"

She looked at Vicky, who didn't even pretend not to be listening.

"In the stairwell, sure." They stepped out onto the narrow platform, and Esther closed the door behind them. She opened her mouth to suggest they go down the stairs to have their chat, but Walter cut her off.

"Are we all right?"

She tried to fake a confused look. "What do you mean?"

"I mean that I called you three times yesterday and you never picked up. I was starting to feel like a stalker. Then I come here to help Adam and I find you've invited everyone else to help but me?"

"I didn't invite everyone," she tried.

Searching

He gave her a knowing look.

She tried to play stupid. It was the only move she could think of.

"I'm sorry if my kiss was presumptuous. I was just so caught up in the joy of the moment."

She didn't know what to say, so said nothing. She imagined Vicky's ear pressed against the other side of the door.

"If you'd prefer it," he said, sounding sad, "I can avoid kissing you in the future."

Oh no. That's not what she wanted. Or was it? She didn't know. She didn't know what to say, but when she looked up into his sad eyes, *she* had the urge to kiss *him*. Of course, she did not, but what was going on with her? She was acting like a silly schoolgirl. She had to say something. "I don't think that's a good idea."

He scowled. "What's not a good idea, kissing you or avoiding kissing you?"

Now she was confused. "I don't think you should avoid kissing me." She gasped at her own forthrightness. "But I am a little overwhelmed. I know that we are moving at a snail's pace, but it still feels fast to me. In so many ways, I still feel like a married woman, and I haven't been courted in a very, very—"

He cut her off by pressing his lips to hers. It occurred to her to pull away, but she didn't. Instead, she let him kiss her, and his lips were warm and comforting.

When *he* pulled away, she wished he hadn't.

"There," he said. "Now that one, I'll admit, I planned. Want to come to my place and watch some television until it's time to get the beans ready?"

She tried to catch her breath. "Let's go to my place. It's much closer, and Zoe is there to chaperon us."

She hadn't been kidding, but Walter laughed all the way down the stairs.

She slowly followed him, her head in the clouds. This was so silly. She was acting like a love-struck teenager. But wait. That wasn't quite true, was it? She stopped descending and thought about it. She *wasn't* feeling like a love-struck teenager. Because she wasn't one. She hadn't felt this way *since* she was a teenager, but she wasn't a teenager now. *Now* she was a woman, a woman who knew the real meaning of love, of relationship, of marriage, of commitment, of friendship. And it was through that glorious, multifaceted lens that she was feeling what she was feeling now. And this feeling, this new thing that God was giving her, well, it was far sweeter than anything she'd felt as a teenager.

Walter stuck his head into the stairwell. "You coming?"

She smiled and started descending again. "Yes, yes. Be patient with me."

He held out his hand. "I promise."

She slid her hand into his, and a warm tingle spread up her arm. Her head started to float again, and she let it soar.

Large Print Books by Robin Merrill

New Beginnings
Knocking
Kicking
Searching
Knitting
Working
Splitting

Shelter Trilogy
Shelter
Daniel
Revival

Piercehaven Trilogy
Piercehaven
Windmills
Trespass

Wing and a Prayer Mysteries
The Whistle Blower
The Showstopper
The Pinch Runner
The Prima Donna

Searching

Gertrude, Gumshoe Cozy Mystery Series
Introducing Gertrude, Gumshoe
Gertrude, Gumshoe: Murder at Goodwill
Gertrude, Gumshoe and the VardSale Villain
Gertrude, Gumshoe: Slam Is Murder
Gertrude, Gumshoe: Gunslinger City
Gertrude, Gumshoe and the Clearwater Curse

Want the inside scoop?
Visit robinmerrill.com to join
Robin's Readers!

Robin also writes sweet romance as Penelope Spark:

Sweet Country Music Romance
The Rising Star's Fake Girlfriend
The Diva's Bodyguard
The Songwriter's Rival

Clean Billionaire Romance
The Billionaire's Cure
The Billionaire's Secret Shoes
The Billionaire's Blizzard
The Billionaire's Chauffeuress
The Billionaire's Christmas